# RETURN OF
# THE MOTHMAN

For Sonia Mae. I miss you.

# RETURN
## OF THE
# MOTHMAN

## MICHAEL KNOST

Woodland Press, LLC

WEST VIRGINIA

III

Woodland Press, LLC

# WOODLAND PRESS

118 Woodland Drive, Chapmanville, WV 25508

# Foreword

*A West Virginia Tapestry*

When I first met Michael Knost, I didn't know that was his real name because he was calling himself Mike Collins for some reason or other. That was the name he'd used when he applied and was accepted for the annual Borderlands Press Writers Boot Camp where I was one of his instructors. As a first-time Grunt, there was no doubt he made a forceful first impression for two reasons: (1.) he was a pretty big guy and you couldn't ignore his presence, and (2.) his writing style was equally burly and muscular.

Although I don't recall the details of the story he submitted to the all-day Saturday round-table of critiques, I do remember his setting was West Virginia, and his characters were all salt-of-the-earth small town folk. The thing that impressed me the most about Michael's writing was how accessible and engaging it was. Even though he was a fairly new writer, he'd already established a narrative voice that was as comfortable to him as an old pair of jeans. Straight from shoulder, not a lot of flash, but easy to read.

Michael was one of those Grunts who came out the other end of the boot camp with a reinforced arsenal of skills and a deeper understanding of how to self-edit and revise his work. He radiated confidence and projected a determination to become a professional writer that was almost palpable. He'd endured some of the boot camp's harsher realities and had become a better writer because he was a tough, quick study.

A few years passed and Michael had kept in touch through the effortless magic of email. When he told me he'd sold a few stories, I knew that, although the curve was steepening, he was going to make it. He validated my faith in him when he told me he was going to be editing an anthology of ghost stories set in his native West Virginia. Its title was *Legends of the Mountain State* and he'd assembled a line-up of equal parts genre vets and talented newcomers. The book was a big seller for its publisher, who has since pressed Michael to continue the series (currently enjoying its 4th volume).

Then he followed it up with an ambitious project entitled *Writers Workshop of Horror*, in which he solicited essays on writing horror fiction from a pool of the best practitioners of the craft—including Clive Barker, Joe Lansdale, F. Paul Wilson, Ramsey Campbell, Rick Hautala, Brian Keene, Gary Braunbeck, and Tim Waggoner. I'm still not sure how Michael did it—other than refusing to take *no* for an answer from all those heavyweights. His persistence and his vision paid off when the book won the 2009 Bram Stoker Award for Non-Fiction at the World Horror Convention in Brighton, England.

In short, Michael Knost has been a non-stop dynamo since blowing the doors off our little genre-publishing redoubt, and he shows no signs of giving any of us much time to re-load before he does it again.

When he asked me to write an introduction to one of his novels, I was of course honored and more than happy to do it. But when I found out it was a novel about the Mothman, I was even more anxious to be a part of the project.

Because me and Mothman go back a long way.

I don't have the space to tell the entire story, especially since I illuminated my connections to the Mothman in both my

M.A.F.I.A. column omnibus collection[1] and also in the After-word to *The Mothman Files* edited by Michael Knost (Hey . . . wait a sec!). Suffice to say that I had met the progenitor of the cultural mythology of the Mothman many years ago—a sincere journalist named John Keel, and have had a soft place in my heart for all things Mothman ever since. In addition, I was very curious to see how Michael had handled the entire corpus of lore concerning the strange flying creature with the bulbous red-glowing eyes.

And I am here to tell you, my friends, he knocked it out of the park.

From the beginning, the entire Mothman Mythos has been owned by West Virginia, and when the stories are told, the trap-pings of the Mountain State are a sizeable part of the larger pic-ture. The Mothman locales are often foreboding, hardscrabble places filled with people not known for fanciful BS. And that's the first thing that struck me about the novel you're itching to read: Michael Knost's innate understanding of West Virginia folks and their towns. *Return of the Mothman* is filled with won-derful characters, most of whom you wish you knew—Ted and his grandmother, the Bear Creek miners, Charles Morgan (as the wise old wizard or wizened scientist), and even the sheriff.

And that's because *not one* character in this book is simply a name on the page. Every one of them has their own story, their own list of joys and horrors that drive them and make them do what they must. As you move through the early chapters and get to know the main players, you like them so much you never wonder when the creature's showing up.

And when we finally meet our nemesis, the first few encoun-ters are brief and teasing because your author knows that less is usually *more*. He gradually ratchets up the dramatic tension and complication by weaving his narrative in and out of each character's troubled life. The effect is subtle and effective, and you're not long into this novel when you realize something very obvious: Michael Knost is a storyteller, plain and simple.

As I was reading this book, I recognized its structure had the feel of the wonderful fifties monster movies I loved so much. Every Saturday afternoon, the theater in our town had a double feature—two black-and-white movies, a cartoon, and something called a "newsreel."[2] Many of the stories hung on a standard plot-skeleton, which introduced all the characters in Act One, the monster in Act Two, and the monster's demise at the end of Act Three. Back then, I think I was only vaguely aware of this classic narrative structure. But I didn't really care or need to know—because it worked! Every Saturday afternoon I watched an endless procession of creature—from *Attack of the Crab Monsters* to *Zontar the Thing from Venus*—all get what they deserved, which was a specially adapted kill-weapon or ju-ju fashioned by the old scientist/folklorist, who just happened to have a beautiful young niece or daughter.

But *Return of the Mothman* is more than a great fifties sci-fi thriller. It's a story about real people dealing with a real terror, a power that is the embodiment of what we mean when we speak of the supernatural. Michael has obviously lived with much of the lore of his monster for quite some time. He's figured the Mothman out, and the novel's *denouement* takes careful measure to logically solve many of the bizarre and often conflicting things we know about the West Virginia horror. His revelation is not only creepy, but also completely plausible.

Okay, I'm gonna wrap this up soon because I don't believe these kinds of preamble to the main heat should be all that windy and cumbersome. I mean, you didn't buy this book because of me, and I don't want to get in the way of the really fun ride you're about to take.

But I did want to take one more line or two to prepare you for perhaps the most important aspect of this book. In fact, it's a vital part of just about everything Michael Knost has ever created, and that's an overwhelming *love* he possesses for his state and its people. As a writer and editor, he's done something only a few others have done, and that's create such well-grounded, believable settings and characters that could only have come from the Mountain State. His stories and anthologies and novels all come together like a country quilt or a tapestry to form a gestalt body of work that is far greater than the sum of its parts.

Maine might lay claim to Stephen King, but West Virginia can't ever be too envious as long as they have Michael Knost in their corner.

—*Tom Monteleone*
*Fallston, MD*

# Prologue

Lenny was too tired to run, and too scared to stop. His lungs burned from the cold, damp mining shafts, his heart pounding his chest. He held a hand over the gash on his forearm trying desperately to contain the bleeding. The light from his helmet bounced and wobbled in front of him with every stride he took. Whether it was the srobing effect, the loss of blood, or the grip of fear in his stomach, he knew dizziness was just the beginning of his troubles.

The screeching from behind him seemed distant, but he was sure the thing would soon be on him again if he didn't hurry. He had to make it back into the regular mining shafts. . . if he could just get back to the broken seal he could probably make it. *A first aid station. Someone's bound to be there to help.*

The thundering grew louder behind him—a beating of enormous wings. The burning scent was growing stronger again, reminding him of his trip to Sulphur Caldron in Yellowstone Park.

Just as he was approaching the broken seal, he tripped on a shoelace or something, sending him skidding to the ground. Sitting up, he noticed the noise had ceased. He pointed the light into the depths from which he'd just came, waiting. Nothing. No screeching. No beating wings. No sounds at all.

He rose to his feet and turned back toward the broken seal. The thing towered over him like a wrestling giant—its red eyes burning into him from the shadows.

Lenny turned the light toward the creature, revealing a blur of teeth and claws as the thing attacked.

XII

# Chapter One

Ted tightened the pungent leather taut over the newly boxed sofa frame and tacked it into place with a staple gun. The material was stiff between his fingers, unwilling to give under the pressure. Smoothing out the wrinkles, he added a few more staples until he could apply finishing nails later. Perspiration beaded his forehead, threatening to run into his eyes. He glanced at his watch, cringing at the thought of waiting another hour before his next smoke break.

"Ted Browning, come to the office, please." The intercom voice was impersonal, generic—the type of voice you hear making announcements at Walmart or Costco.

He placed the stapler next to a box of spacers on the workbench. *Now what?* He'd clocked in late maybe twice during his eighteen years at Mott Furniture Manufacturing, and he'd never missed a quota.

He was cutting fabric for the North Carolina company at the age of twenty-two before working his way up to assembly within a year. *It's about that scratched dresser.* He rubbed the back of his neck. *I told the lumber guys not to stack loose material too close to finished products.*

He patted his shirt pocket to ensure the pack of Marlboro's was still there, and then headed for the stairwell leading up to the main office. His footsteps echoed from the metal rungs with cavernous depth.

The management offices overlooked the assembly floor with mirrored windows so the workers never knew when, or if, someone was watching them. The upper level always seemed colder than the rest of the building, which was odd as heat is known to rise.

He pressed a hand against his stomach to ease the queasiness. *What is wrong with me?*

Pausing just outside the main office door, he searched his pockets for something to freshen his breath, finding only loose change and the Zippo that Rosalina gave him during their last Christmas together. He quickly flipped it over and ran a thumb across the engraving. *Your Flame Forever - Lina.* He turned the doorknob, pushed through.

Inside, the secretary was on the phone, explaining sick leave to a caller. Ted waited in front of the woman's desk, trying not to look as if he was eavesdropping on her conversation.

"I'm sorry, but if you take three sick days in a row," she repeated, "you are required to have a doctor's excuse." She gestured toward the receiver and rolled her eyes. "I'm sorry, that's company policy. Thank you for calling." She smiled at Ted. "I honestly don't see how some people make it from day to day." She gazed over the wire rim glasses perched on the end of her nose. "The level of stupidity I have to deal with on a daily basis is ridiculous."

Ted offered a nervous grin.

"I'm sorry to keep you waiting." She cleaned the phone's receiver with a Clorox wipe. "What can I do for you?"

"I'm Ted Browning." The words came out more as a question than a statement.

"Oh, you have a phone call."

He stared at her for a moment. "Are you sure it's for me?"

Nodding, she pressed one of the buttons on the console and held the handset out to him. "Here you go."

Bleach fumes reached his nostrils before the receiver touched the side of his face. "Hello?" A series of high-pitched tones amid thick static caused him to jerk the handset away. It was like a fax connection but the tones were different. When the noises subsided, he returned the handset to his ear, detecting a distinct rustling over the static. "Hello?"

Low and raspy whispers echoed in the receiver. The hairs on his arms reacted, sending a chill through his back and neck. Something wasn't right about these whispers—something stilted, weird.

"Who is this?"

More rustling before the dial tone abruptly sounded.

"Is everything okay?" The secretary's painted eyebrows gathered over the bridge of her nose. "You look as pale as a ghost."

Ted paused before returning the handset to her. "Must have been a bad connection."

"Well, what did they say?"

"I'm not sure." He stared past her. "There was a lot of noise and—"

"You couldn't understand what they said?"

Warmth tingled his cheeks. "It sounded like someone

3

said, '*Your grandmother needs you.*'"

"Oh my." She held her gaze to his while dabbing at the receiver with another wipe. "Is your grandmother sick?"

"Could I use the phone again? I'll pay whatever charges come up."

"Don't worry about that," she said, handing the receiver back to him.

It took four rings before a familiar voice answered. It wasn't the voice he expected, although he always thought his cousin sounded like his grandmother—a younger version, of course, and not as feisty.

"Is that you, Kim?"

"Where are you?"

He moved the handset from one ear to the next, turning his back to the staring secretary. "Did you just try to call me on a bad connection?"

"No, I didn't know how to contact you. Where are you?"

"I'm at work." Bile crept into his esophagus. "Where's Gran?"

"You need to come home."

"That doesn't tell me anything, Kim."

"She's in the hospital. I just dropped by to pick up a few things for her."

"Is she okay?"

"She's sleeping right now." Drawers opened and closed in the background. "They gave her something to help her sleep."

He ran a hand through his hair. "What happened?"

"She called Mom this morning complaining about stomach pain while working in her rose garden. She started spitting up blood so we rushed her to the emergency room."

Ted's intestines wrapped around his stomach, squeezing, kneading. "How long has she been there?"

"A few hours."

"Be honest with me," he said, closing his eyes. "How bad—"

"You'd better get here soon."

## Chapter Two

The pickup's tire tread hummed against the asphalt, a monotonous roar tempting Ted with sleep. He'd opened the driver's side window half an inch, hoping the night air, along with the blasting radio, would keep him awake. Instead, he found it only made him both sleepy *and* cold.

There didn't seem to be another vehicle on the road, which was relaxing as heavy traffic always wrecked his nerves. In fact, the muscles in his stomach still ached from rush-hour gridlock. It was as if he'd been working out with the abs-buster machine he now used as a clothing rack.

*I should have visited her more.* He drew on the cigarette, allowing its cherry to burn into the filter before stubbing it out in the overflowing ashtray. Smoke swirled the cab, burning his eyes. *She never let on that anything was wrong.*

Pink Floyd's "Another Brick in the Wall" blared from the speakers, bass notes reverberating into his chest. He'd found the classic rock station after crossing into Virginia only to realize the music of his past evoked memories he wished would remain buried.

He shook another Marlboro from its pack and gently lipped it before pulling the red and white box away. The trip home was usually a five-hour drive, but it looked as though he'd make it to Logan, West Virginia, in record time.

He couldn't stand the thought of losing his grand-mother—she was all he had left. In fact, he couldn't even imagine her in a weak or dependent state. "If you show signs of weakness, folks will walk all over you," he re-membered her saying. It must have been good advice be-cause no one ever walked on Myrtle Browning. Ever.

He lit the cigarette, drawing deeply. The nicotine was as soothing as Calamine lotion on a weeping rash of poi-son ivy. *How old is she getting to be now?* She was thirty-seven when his parents died in the accident—he'd just turned two. *So that makes her what, seventy-five?*

The lifeless road ahead was a tunnel of darkness, re-minding him of the murky mineshaft he'd worked in be-fore moving to North Carolina. He cranked up the heater, turned off the radio, and forced his thoughts away from the dark crevices.

The bell over the door rang as Ted entered the Squire To-bacco Unlimited. The foyer was small with a number of items close to the counter and cash register. The walls were covered with cigar signs and framed photographs of loyal customers. To the right, through a glass door, a small group sat around a coffee table in brown leather sofas and chairs, puffing away on cigars.

"Oh my gosh," Charlie Morgan said, stepping out of the walk-in humidor. His smile was enormous. "Ted Browning? Is that you?"

Ted grinned. "In the flesh."

Charlie hugged Ted and led him into the lounge. "Hey, everyone, I want to introduce you to someone special. This guy was one of my earliest customers." He put his arm around Ted, careful not to allow the cigar to get too close. "I probably would have gone out of business the first year were it not for him and a handful of other faithfuls."

The cigar shop was a place Ted frequented with Jeff after high school. They usually searched for girls while walking around in the Town Center Mall, caught a movie, and then kicked back with a cigar at Charlie's place.

Ted laughed. "It's good to see you."

"Let me introduce everyone to you." Charlie gestured to the others. "This is Brian Hatcher, Grace Welch, Todd Reynolds, and Mike Collins."

Ted nodded to each individual as Charlie called their names. "Nice to meet all of you."

"Let me buy you a cigar," Charlie said, walking toward the humidor. It seemed bigger than it was during the days he and Jeff plundered it nearly every Saturday. "Anything in particular? Wait, you loved Romeo Julieta, Churchill, right?"

"That's right. You have a great memory." Ted held his hands up. "But I can't stay, I just stopped by to pick up a few on my way into Logan."

"Are you sure?"

"Yeah," Ted said. "Just surprise me with a few you think I'll like."

"What's your hurry?"

Ted shook his head. "Gran's in the hospital."

"Oh, I hope it's nothing serious."

"I'm hoping the same," Ted said. "As of this moment,

no one seems to be able to tell me anything."

"There's not too much that can keep Myrtle down, she's a tough cookie."

"Don't I know it," Ted said.

Charlie was gone but a minute before bringing back three large cigars in a Ziploc bag. "I wanted to give you a variety," he said, handing the bag to Ted. "Let me know what you think of the Partagas, it's a new one."

"I will," Ted said, reaching for his wallet. "I need one of those plastic cutters, too."

"Here you go," Charlie said, retrieving one from behind the counter.

"How much do I owe you?"

Charlie held his hands up. "On the house."

"You don't have to do that."

"I know I don't have to, but I want to."

"Well I appreciate the generosity," Ted said. "Thank you."

Charlie grinned. "Just don't wait another twenty years for your next visit, okay?"

"You got it. Thanks again."

The sun peeked over the hazy mountaintops as Ted took the familiar exit. The bare trees, normally clothing the mountains with a patchwork of colors this time of year, revealed a tarnished carpet of decaying leaves. The branches swayed with the wind, bowing and clacking against one another.

He couldn't believe how little Logan County had changed since he'd left—other than the ongoing deterioration of buildings and roads. He pulled onto the hospital grounds, parking the truck at the far side of the lot. The enormous building, although now slightly remodeled, was the same one he'd been born in. "You were the talk of the staff," his grandmother often bragged. "All the nurses wanted to take you home."

A frail woman wearing a pink smock was dozing at the front desk when he stepped inside the foyer. The sound of the automatic doors startled her awake. "Can I help you?"

"I need the room number for Myrtle Browning?"

The woman looked as old as the hospital itself, her mauve-tinted hair was hair sprayed into the shape of a football helmet.

"Myrtle Browning," she repeated, scanning hand-written names on the sheet of paper in front of her. "Ah, here it is, room 317."

The elevator smelled of gauze and pine cleaner yet offered little in the way of a sterile environment. Magic marker graffiti bled through a thin coat of white paint, revealing professions of love and vulgarity. Ted was thankful the overhead speaker was silent, as he certainly wasn't in the mood for easy listening versions of pop trash.

The car stopped at the second floor with a jerk, a muffled ding sounding from the other side of the wall. Before the doors could fully open, a disheveled man wearing a loose-fitting hospital gown stormed in, grabbing at Tom's jacket.

"We're all going to die!" The old man's eyes were wild, rheumy. "He's ready to finish it!"

Ted tried pushing him away, but found the grip too strong to break. The doors were just ready to close when two nurses rushed in to help. "Now, Mister Callaway," the tallest woman said, reaching for him. "You need to get back in your bed, you've had another episode."

The man's arms tightened around Ted like a hungry anaconda, squeezing tighter with every exhalation of its prey. The man pushed his face within an inch of Ted's. "He's out there, somewhere! He's come back!" Ted winced at the man's breath, a potpourri of vomit and halitosis.

"You're getting yourself worked up again, Mr. Callaway, and you know that's not good for your heart." The nurse pulled at the old man's arms while the other woman tugged at his waist.

"Don't you people understand? He's come back! And this time he plans to finish what he started!"

"It's all right, Mr. Callaway," the tallest woman said. "We're safe inside the hospital."

The man turned back to Ted. "No one is safe. No one!"

The nurses finally pried the man away, apologizing as they struggled to remove him from the elevator car. His screams echoed from the hall even after the doors closed.

It wasn't until the elevator started moving again that Ted realized he was shaking. There was another muffled ding before the doors reopened to an empty waiting room. He stepped into the dimly lit corridor stretching out in both directions.

His footsteps echoed from the glossy tile, unease still clinging to him like damp clothing. A yellowing florescent light buzzed overhead. Waylon Jennings was faintly describing the latest trouble Bo and Luke Duke found themselves in as an episode of *The Dukes of Hazard* boomed from somewhere within the recessed nursing station.

A broad woman sat grinning at a small television, face awash in screen light. Tootsie Roll wrappers littered the desktop in front of her, each folded in neat squares. It was obvious she had a few pieces in her mouth. "Can I help you?" she said, her gaze never leaving the Duke boys.

"I'm looking for room 317."

"Second door on the right," she said, gesturing toward one end of the hall.

Ted paused at the door, wondering if he should knock or discreetly slip inside. Quietude closed in, smothering him. He envisioned his grandmother bedfast with wires, hoses, and oxygen machines overwhelming her frail body. The cold metal of the door handle penetrated his hand, coursing blue waves into his arm.

He finally pushed inside, finding an ill-lit room with a few machines surrounding the elevated bed where his grandmother lay. A single line ran from an IV bag to the back of her hand where the needle was secured with a few strips of bandage tape.

Movement from the corner of the room caught his attention when his cousin Kim rose from a straight-back visitor's chair.

She hugged him, leaning her head against his. "She's been asleep for about an hour."

"How is she?"

"Let's go outside so we don't wake her." She nodded toward the door. "'Sides, I'm dying for a smoke."

Ted cupped his hands around a Marlboro, trying to shield the wind from the lighter's flame. He kept the Zippo in his hand just in case he'd need it again. "So, no test results yet?"

"None so far," Kim said, exhaling bluish smoke.

He paused a moment, giving her time to volunteer insights on Myrtle's hospital visit before moving on. "How's Earl?"

"He's fine, other than workin' hisself to death."

"Yeah? He still on the hoot-owl at Bear Creek?"

"Lord, yes." She rolled her eyes. "Especially since most of the men are too spooked to work late. Course, we need the money so Earl's taking all the overtime he can get."

"Spooked?"

Kim smiled around a cigarette drawl. "Yeah, apparently some of the men are hearing noises that are freakin' 'em out."

"What kind of noises?"

Kim shrugged. "Some say it's a massive pounding. Others say it's a distant wind. I think it's a ploy to get on an earlier shift." She dropped the cigarette butt, stepping on it. "I'd better get to work. How long you plan on stayin'?"

"As long as it takes, I guess."

"I'll stop back by after work." She twirled a set of keys on her forefinger. "Call the restaurant if you need anything." She hugged him again before walking off toward the parking lot.

Easing into the bedside chair, Ted noticed Myrtle's labored, shallow breathing. He pulled up closer, taking out his deck of cards, and began laying them out on the bed for a game of solitaire. *I should have been here.*

The cards warmed his hands as he moved them from stock to cascades to foundations with confidence and fluidity. *I would have noticed something was wrong and talked her into seeing the doctor sooner.* The quiet of the room relaxed his mind, causing his eyelids to droop. Pangs of guilt washed over him while unpleasant memories tried to creep in. He did his best to shake off sleep, but found keeping his eyelids open a difficult task.

The darkness moved, souring Ted's stomach as he attempted to identify the noise growing closer, louder. He knew he was dreaming, and that fact alone made the experience even weirder. The noise almost sounded like wings beating the air, but the incredible amount of stirred wind would have required enormous wings, far larger than anything his mind could comprehend. The sourness festered, causing cold sweat to sheen his face and neck.

He strained his eyes in the lightlessness, focusing on illusions the darkness conjured. His heart pounded his chest, a caged animal trying to escape an approaching predator. His hands gripped at his soaked shirt, pressing it against goose flesh. Somehow he could sense something was moving toward him. The presence was significant, jarring, giving rise to a level of apprehension he'd never experienced.

*Something is coming.* That's all his fevered mind could produce. *Something evil.* It was as if some internal detector had just pegged the extreme, offering a spiritual awakening, a warning, hope of escape.

Then he saw the glowing red eyes.

## Chapter Three

Ted awakened to the scent of oatmeal and toast, shielding his eyes from the morning lights. He rolled his head about his shoulders, hoping to work the stiffness out of his neck.

"Well, it's about time you woke up," his grandmother said from the hospital bed. "When did you get in?"

"A couple of hours ago." He struggled to read the hands on his Timex. "Are you feeling all right?"

"I've seen better days, I reckon." She pushed thickened oatmeal around the bowl, mixing the crusty edges into its gooey center. "Seen better food, too."

"Well, you might as well get used to it," he said, collecting the scattered playing cards from the bed. "You're probably going to be here a while."

She leaned forward. "We'll see about that."

"You know they'll want to at least monitor you a few days."

"You mark my words on this." She pointed an arthritic finger at him. "I'll be leaving this hospital *today*." Settling back into the pillows, she folded her arms across her chest, beaming with defiance.

Ted knew it was pointless to press the issue as he was certain he'd inherited her stubborn gene. "You beat everything, you know that?"

"Why don't you make yourself useful and sneak

some goodies in here from the candy machines?"

"You know I can't do that."

She rolled her eyes. "Ain't nothin' stoppin' you but *you*."

"So, why have you been hiding your health issues from me?"

"You gonna make me get out of this bed and find the machines myself?"

Ted bit his tongue, closed his eyes, breathed. "We have to wait and see what the doctor says before turning you loose with junk food."

"It don't matter what the doctor says, Teddy. When it's my time to go, I want my belly filled with sweets." She held up a spoonful of the congealed oatmeal. "Not lumpy wallpaper paste."

He rubbed the back of his neck. "Let me see what I can do."

She pointed toward the nightstand. "Get my purse out of that drawer and I'll give you some quarters."

"Don't worry, I'll take care of it."

"No." She nodded forcefully at the nightstand. "I've got a whole mess of change you can use."

Ted estimated the fading purse's age at least twenty years old. . . the only one he remembered her owning. "Are you carrying bricks in this thing?"

"You're 'bout as funny as you've never been."

Ted shook his head. "Where in the world do you come up with your sayings?"

"Old timey talk," she said rummaging through the purse. "I guess I'm a dinosaur ready for extinction." She handed him several quarters, winking. "Tyrannosaurus Redneck."

Ted chuckled. "Well, at least you've still got your sense of humor."

"Don't tell Doc Hamilton. Lord knows he'll either want to remove it or give me a pill for it." She shook her head. "These doctors don't want you to die, but they sure don't want you to live, either."

Ted moved for the door, pausing momentarily at the foot of her bed. "BBQ chips, right?"

Her eyes sparkled. "And a Milky Way bar."

The vending machines looked as though they'd been attacked by savages—banged up, half empty, and abandoned. The few remaining items, mostly licorice sticks and chewing gum, were surrounded by empty sections. He dropped a few quarters in the slot and punched in the combination D-4, which put a large spring into motion, pushing a Hershey bar over the edge and into the waiting bin below.

"Pathetic, isn't it?" A man wearing a starched Polo shirt with a stethoscope dangling from his neck stood just behind him.

"Excuse me?" Ted said.

The man gestured toward the machines. "They're always bare."

Ted squinted at the man's name badge.

"I'm Dr. Hamilton. You must be Ted."

Ted fingered a button on his shirt. "Do I know you?"

"Let's just say your grandmother loves showing off

photographs of you."

"I'm sorry about that." Ted's cheeks warmed. "She's used to getting her way and doesn't usually think of others."

"Quite all right, my mother does the exact same thing with me."

Ted smiled. "In fact, she's talked me into sneaking something in for her from the vending machines." He rubbed his chin with the back of his hand. "I know I shouldn't do it, but she has a way of—"

"Let her have anything she wants."

Ted paused, blinking. "What's that?"

"Give her whatever she wants." He lowered his gaze. "Now's not the time to be concerned with healthy choices."

Ted stepped away from the machine. "What are you saying?"

"The test results are not good." He finally met his gaze. "I'm afraid your grandmother has terminal cancer."

Ted placed a hand over his mouth, thinking he would vomit. "Are you sure?"

"It started in her stomach, but the tests show it's now in her liver." He shook his head. "Too far gone by the time she got here."

"So, how long does she have?"

"It's hard to say, but if the cancer continues to progress as it has, I'd guess six months." He placed a hand on Ted's shoulder. "I'm sorry."

Ted didn't want to speak, didn't want to be around anyone at the moment—all he wanted to do was sink to the floor, sobbing. Instead, he cleared his throat, straightened his back. "Does she know?"

"I'm on my way to tell her now."

Ted recognized the icy fingers of shock clutching his body—they were the same fingers that squeezed the breath from him the day Jeff died. "All right," he said, not knowing what to do with the candy bar. "I'll go with you."

Myrtle was in the middle of a coughing fit when Ted and Doctor Hamilton entered the room. Her eyes looked as though they were bulging from the pressure. "Get her some water," Hamilton said to Ted. He pressed the nurse button beside the bed before placing the stethoscope buds in his ears.

"Can I help you?" The voice from the intercom sounded tired, stressed.

"This is Doctor Hamilton." He reached for the clipboard. "Mrs. Browning needs Codiclear for cough sedation."

There was a pause from the intercom before the voice spoke again, this time sounding energetic. "How many milligrams?"

"Five will be fine." He pressed the stethoscope's diaphragm against her chest. "I need that as soon as possible."

"On my way."

Ted nearly spilled the water as he filled a styrofoam cup from the bedside pitcher. "Here you go," he said, handing it to Myrtle.

She drank deeply, her chest heaving while recovering

lost breath. Wiping tears from her eyes, she emptied the cup. "You two look as nervous as a couple of long-tailed cats in a room full of rockin' chairs."

The nurse entered, moving quickly to Myrtle's side. "Is it all right to give this to her now?"

"Yes, and check her blood pressure, too."

"You all are showin' me an awful lot of attention," Myrtle said, volleying her gaze from Dr. Hamilton to Ted.

"We need to talk, Ms. Browning." Doctor Hamilton pulled the chair closer to the bed, easing into it. "Your test results came back."

She lifted her eyebrows. "And?"

"Well, the results are not good. Unfortunately, the cancer has spread to your liver."

She coughed into a tissue. "What does that mean?"

"It puts you in Stage-4." He glanced at Ted before continuing. "I'm afraid it's terminal."

She stared at her hands a few moments before finally turning to Ted, smiling. "I told you I'd be goin' home today."

## Chapter Four

Coal Branch hollow's one-lane road was riddled with potholes and bumps—contours of rocks and debris barely covered with a thin layer of asphalt. The scent of horse manure penetrated the truck cab, reminding Ted of 4-H camp.

"Been a while since I've traveled these roads," he said.

"I wish you'd drive 'em more often." Myrtle held her gaze out the passenger side window. "But I understand you got to work."

"Has Tom Pritchard moved away?" He jutted his chin toward a dilapidated house as they passed by it. "Looks like his grass is taking over the place."

Myrtle faced him. "Honey, Tom died several months back. Black lung kept him in failin' health for years." She shifted her gaze back out the window. "I reckon this whole hollow's been dyin' for a while now."

Ted wanted to say something, but couldn't find the words.

"I hate that you had to come all the way back here on account of me bein' sick and all."

He rubbed his jawline with a thumb. "Long overdue."

"You can only do so much, Teddy."

The inclining road veered to the right, running parallel with a small, winding creek. The further they drove, the fewer houses dotted the creek bank, seemingly replaced by encroaching poplars and firs. Dead branches cluttered the landscape, skeletons of a harsh Fall.

"Must have been an awful big storm to make such a mess of things," Ted said.

"Aw, most of these trees are diseased, it wouldn't take much of a wind to knock those branches off."

The old home place came into view, its surrounding shrubs and bushes appearing as lifeless as the slumbering house. Paint chips littered the shaggy lawn like dandruff, leaving dry, discolored splotches on the wood siding. Ted put the truck into park and patted his shirt pocket. "Hang on, I'll come around and help you."

"I ain't crippled," Myrtle said, gathering her belongings. "I can make it on my own just fine."

Ted gently took her hand. "Let me do this." His voice lowered to a whisper. "Please?"

Her hard expression melted. "All right, if it'll make you feel better."

"It will."

The scent of linoleum and homemade quilts overwhelmed Ted as he helped her into the house—at least those were the first things that came to mind when the aromas of home met them at the door. Myrtle's full weight burdened his arm, a clear sign she would never have made it inside on her own.

"Let's get you settled in," he said, leading her to the recliner. "And then I'll go get something from McDonald's. Does that sound all right to you?"

"Now you're talkin'!"

Ted chuckled at the voice of the Myrtle Browning of his youth. "I thought that might perk you up."

Her cold grip tightened on Ted's arms while he eased her into the chair. She stared up at him, grimacing. "What time did they say hospice would be here?"

"Sometime after four o'clock."

"Well, it's pert near three now." She dabbed a wadded tissue at her mouth, obvious attempts at concealing the wheeze. "You'd better be goin' so you can get back in time to help 'em when they get here."

"You want your usual?"

"Do you even remember what my usual is?"

Ted crossed his arms over his chest, grinning. "Big Mac without the salad dressing, large fries, and a bucket of Dr. Pepper?"

"And tell 'em I don't want a whole head of lettuce shredded on my burger!"

"Anything else?"

"Hang on a second," she said, rummaging through her purse. "Let me give you some money."

"Do you need ketchup?"

"Lord no." She handed him a twenty. "Their ketchup tastes like somebody stuffed tomatoes into a twelve-gauge shotgun and blasted 'em into whatever they fill those packets with."

Ted chuckled. "You're downright poetic at times, you know that?"

"Poetry in motion," she said, pointing toward the coffee table. "Hand me the flicker before you leave."

"So, you'll be all right while I'm gone?"

She glared up at him. "I promise not to die in the next thirty minutes or so, if that's what you're worried about."

"You know what I mean." He scratched his forehead. "I just worry about you."

"I know, Teddy." Her frail smile revealed dentures that looked abnormally large in her emaciated face. "I'll be fine."

"Well, I should be back in just a few minutes."

"Here," she said, digging in her purse again. "You might as well take the telephone you got me for emergencies." She rolled her eyes. "You do know how to *use* one, don't you?"

"I don't need—"

"Take it," she said, shaking the small flip phone at him. "If I have to get a hold of you, I don't want to wait."

Outside, Ted climbed into the truck cab, half expecting to find Myrtle standing at the living room window, pulling back the curtains. Instead, shadows formed from the ceiling fan rotated among the flickering television light.

He closed his hand around the phone, wanting to smash it into the dashboard. Taking a deep breath, he opened the phone and began dialing. The monotonous ringing in the receiver seemed far away, muffled.

"Hello, this is Ted Browning," he said when a woman finally answered. "I'm not going to be able to come back to work." He pinched the bridge of his nose. "No, my grandmother is sick and needs me." Staring at the living room window, he ended the connection and took out a Marlboro. "I need a drink."

The hospice nurse arrived an hour and a half later, smiling far more than what seemed appropriate for someone working under the auspices of death. A couple of men delivered a truckload of home-bound amenities, including a hospital bed—which Myrtle swore she'd never use.

Ted took advantage of the time the nurse spent tending to Myrtle by stepping out onto the porch for a smoke. A brilliant cardinal rested on the rock wall that stretched around the back of the house. It flew away at the first flick of Ted's lighter, disappearing into the copse of bare trees on the mountainside.

Another gust of wind washed over him, carrying the scent of pine needles and rain. Tree branches swayed hypnotically like enticing sirens, enchanting anyone unlucky enough to pass by.

Ted was halfway through the cigarette when a growling muffler echoed through the valley. There were benefits to living in the last house on the hollow—one of the biggest was vantage point. He recognized his cousin Kim and her husband Earl in the familiar Ford F-150 as they pulled up the driveway.

Earl opened the driver's side door before allowing the truck to come to a complete stop. "Kim told me you were in," he said, climbing down. "I had to stop by and see you. Can't stay long, though. I'm heading to work."

"Good to see you, Earl."

Kim stepped onto the porch. "How's she doing?"

"Not too good." Ted rubbed an eyebrow. "It's terminal cancer."

She stood motionless, tears leaving pale streaks in her makeup.

Ted struggled with the silence. "She's in good spirits."

Kim buried her face into his neck, wrapping boney arms around his shoulders. "What do the doctors know?" Her breath warmed his skin, her tears chilling his soul. "She'll probably outlive us all."

Ted finally rested a hand on her back. "Well, the way I smoke, that probably wouldn't be too big of a deal."

She dabbed at tears, laughing. "I could say the same about my chocolate addiction."

"And my beer," Earl added with a decayed grin.

"Hospice is here right now. They've got a hospital bed set up, but we're going to have a fight on our hands getting her in it."

"I'll ask Mom to stop by. She'll get her in the bed. Are you going to be here a while?"

"I'm here for the long haul," Ted said, shifting his gaze to the tree line.

"What about your job?"

He jutted a thumb toward the house. "She's my full-time job now."

"And your stuff in North Carolina?"

"I guess I'll have to move it all here."

"If you need any help with that, let me know," Earl said. "I'm off tomorrow and the next day."

"Thanks, but I think I can manage on my own."

"And I can take off a few days to stay with Myrtle while you're gone," Kim said.

"I appreciate it, but—"

"Then it's settled." Kim turned to Earl. "You need to find out how much Gary can get a U-Haul for." She turned back to Ted. "Earl's brother rents 'em at his gas station, so we should be able to get a good deal on one."

"Well, I'm gonna have to scoot," Earl said, checking his watch. "Don't want to be late for work. I'll give you a call to let you know what Gary says."

Ted tossed the cigarette into the yard. "Thanks, but—"

"No buts," Kim said, wrapping her arms around him. "You don't have to do this alone."

He focused his attention to the fluttering red in his peripheral vision, finding the cardinal back on the wall with a fat night crawler squirming in its beak. "Thanks."

After a small supper of soup and sandwiches, Ted placed a kitchen chair beside Myrtle. He was amazed that Aunt Dorothy was able to get her into the hospital bed. "You hardly touched your sandwich," he said, collecting the dishes.

"I haven't had much of an appetite lately."

"Well, you need to eat." He tucked the box of crackers under his arm. "You have to maintain your strength."

"They that wait upon the Lord shall renew their strength." She laid a hand on the worn Bible at her side. "They shall mount up as eagle's wings. They shall run and not grow weary, and they shall walk and not faint."

"If you're going to beat this, you'll need calories to go along with your faith."

"The strength He promises is not strength for this world." She pointed upward, offering a sympathetic smile. "And I've laid up my treasures far from here."

Ted rose from the chair. "Just don't give up so easily on the here and now."

"I'm not giving up anything, Teddy," she said, reaching for his free hand. "I'm just ready to go."

"Listen," he said. "You can beat this."

"To be absent from the body is to be present with the Lord." She squeezed his hand. "You can't beat *that*."

Ted eased onto the edge of the bed. "What am I going to do with you?"

A smile tightened the wrinkles around her mouth. "Let me go," she said with a wink. "That's all you can do."

Ted stared at their hands.

"I know it's hard for you, Teddy." She leaned into him. "Letting go seems to be something you've been forced to do your whole life. First your momma and daddy, then Jeff."

Ted cleared his throat, rose from the bed. "I'd better get these dishes washed."

She refused to let go of his hand. "Wait a second."

"I need to—"

"Them dishes can wait." She nodded sternly toward the chair. "Sit."

Ted slipped his right hand into his pocket and eased onto the bedside. "I know what you're—"

"Are you still laborin' those thoughts?" The bed moaned as she struggled to sit up. "You know Jeff's death wasn't your fault."

29

He slipped his fingers around the odd coin in his pocket. "I don't—"

"There wasn't a thing you could have done." She shook her head. "You know it, and I know it. Just because you were assigned to the same section doesn't mean you should have died, too."

Ted let his shoulders go slack, allowing her to speak uninterrupted.

"You're alive, Teddy—for God's sake, *live!*"

The warmth in his cheeks spread to his earlobes. "I know." He stroked her speckled knuckles. "I know."

The silence was suffocating. Myrtle just stared out the window, her face awash in moonlight. "I'd give anything to see my roses." She smiled at something unseen. "Your Great Grandpa built that rock wall when I was just a little girl. He said it was to keep deer and other varmints out of the garden." She turned to face Ted. "Gardens were for survival back in those days, not like today's hobbies."

"I always wondered why you planted your roses outside the wall."

"I didn't. Momma put 'em there before Daddy built the wall."

"You're kidding? How long have they been there?"

"My guess would be 'round eighty years." Her eyes brightened. "The key is plenty of watering, pruning, and mulching."

"Oh, I know the hours you've spent with them."

"*Cultivating relationships,* Momma called it." Her smile widened. "They're like old friends."

Ted studied the rock wall. "I could open up the section in front of the roses if you wanted."

"No, honey, you don't have to do that."

"I've got a lot of memories of that wall," he said, gazing out the window. "We played cowboys and Indians on it, pretending to defend Fort Browning."

Myrtle chuckled. "Poor Jeff always wanted to play the general, but you never would let him." Her laughter spurred a few coughs. "And he *hated* playing an Injun."

"Those were the good old days." Ted realized he was smiling and wiped his mouth. "I think it would be nice to see the roses from here, if you ask me."

"Now Teddy—"

"Seriously, I want to do it."

Myrtle held her probing gaze to his face. "It's fine with me," she said, allowing her smile to return. "Just be careful, those rocks are much heavier than they look."

"Don't worry, I can handle it."

## Chapter Five

The crossword puzzle was the quietest thing Ted could find to occupy his mind while waiting for Kim and Earl to arrive. He didn't want to wake up Myrtle, and it was too cold for him to wait on the porch. Since Kim wasn't specific with details during last night's late call, Ted wasn't sure if she and Earl would show up in a U-Haul truck, or if he and Earl would get one on the way to North Carolina.

The morning dew left a glistening sheen over the valley as sunlight peeked through murky clouds. He checked off the clue he'd just answered and moved on to twenty-three down. *A nocturnal bird that begins with the letter O.*

Growling gears grew louder from outside, prompting him to peek out the front door. A white and orange box truck emerged from the road's final bend. He could see Earl and Kim bouncing in the cab as the U-Haul lumbered up the driveway.

Owl.

Satisfied Myrtle was still asleep, he slipped out to the front porch.

"How's it going?" Kim said, climbing down from the truck cab.

"It was a rough night, but she's sleeping now."

"Well, don't worry about a thing. I'll take care of her."

Ted checked his pockets for keys and cigarettes. "I don't doubt that a bit."

"We'd better hit the road, man," Earl said from the truck. "We're gonna want to beat the morning traffic."

"Be right there." Ted turned back to Kim. "I have Myrtle's cell phone if you need to get in touch with me for anything."

"All right," she said, pushing him toward the steps. "Now get going before Earl starts blowin' the horn."

He paused at the edge of the porch. "Thanks, Kim."

She smiled. "Make sure Earl stays awake while driving."

"I thought he only gets sleepy when he's drinking."

Kim raised an eyebrow. "Exactly."

"Great. That's all I need."

"Just make him think he spilled beer while paying attention to the road." She gave him a sneaky grin. "He'll have you in the driver's seat for the rest of the trip."

Ted laughed. "Because spilling beer is alcohol abuse to Earl."

"You boys be careful."

Ted caught a whiff of wintergreen Skoal as he climbed into the cab, which reminded him of his first few months working in the mines as a red hat. He was little more than a kid back then, just out of high school, soaking in every piece of advice the old hands had to offer. So when Leo Anderson suggested chewing tobacco helped keep coal dust out of a miner's lungs, Ted picked up the snuff habit like most of the younger guys. He didn't give it up until a few years after moving to North Carolina. And even then, it was more of trading tobacco habits—snuff for cigarettes.

Earl lifted a Budweiser can to his lips. "Ready?" Just when it appeared he would take a sip, he spat a stream of amber into the pop-top opening.

Ted gazed at the Coleman cooler next to Earl's feet. "You all right to drive?"

A wrinkled cigarette jutted from behind Earl's ear, partially hidden by a thick mane of hair nearly touching his shoulders. "Never better."

"All right," Ted said. "Winston-Salem, here we come."

"Git 'er done."


The U-Haul's empty bay rattled against the highway's steady hum, making conversation nearly impossible. Ted stared out the window, watching the mountains atrophy with distance and time.

"Kim tells me you're working the hoot-owl."

"Yeah, I'm wracking up overtime." Earl took a beer from the cooler and held it out to Ted.

"No, thanks."

"Not too many are willing to work the night shift," Earl said, opening the can. "I ain't never seen such a bunch of cowards in all my life."

"Kim told me something about that."

"You know how it is, man, you've worked underground." He shook his head. "You're gonna hear things, you're gonna see things, it's part of working in darkness and isolation."

"Ain't that the truth."

"It all started when Lenny Morton disappeared. You

remember Lenny, he'd go anywhere in the mines, he didn't care." He shook his head. "Ever since then the men have complained about hearing strange things, and even seeing 'em."

"What are they saying they've seen?"

"Something flyin' around the east entrance, something huge." He took a long drink. "And somethin' about noises near section eleven."

"Kim mentioned that—something about it sounding like—"

"The Mothman."

Ted studied his face. "What?"

"That's what they're sayin'. . . the men." His grin revealed the clump of snuff behind his bottom lip. "They're sayin' it's the Mothman."

"Are you serious?"

"A few guys have even said they've seen glowing eyes inside section eleven."

Ted tried concealing the shiver running down his back. "Sounds like a few pillbillies on the job if you ask me."

"Apparently the company thought the same thing. They implemented a company-wide drug test."

"And?"

"Three fellas popped positive, none of which had claimed seeing anything."

Ted rubbed his forehead. "That's strange."

"What, that that many people have claimed seeing something?"

"No, that so few of the men popped positive on a

drug test."

"I'm with you on that," Earl said, laughing.

The scenery flashed by as Ted stared out the passenger window; nameless landscapes rolled past, populated by faceless people.

"So, does all this talk have the company looking to do any hiring?"

"They're always looking for people, especially when it comes to experienced fellas like yourself."

"You can forget that." Ted crossed his arms. "Myrtle would kill me if I ever stepped foot into another mine."

"I'm just sayin' they'd hire you in a heartbeat. You remember Jerry Price, don't you?"

"Yeah, we went through certification together."

"Well, he's the nightshift foreman now. He wanted me to tell you that you have a job waiting for you when you're ready."

Ted smiled. "Jerry's a good guy, but I'm done with mining."

"He told me you'd say that, but wanted you to know the offer stands."

"Tell him I appreciate it but Jerry, of all people, knows why I can't do it."

"He told me you would say that, too."

"Is that right?" Ted scratched his chin. "What else did he tell you?"

"That it's going to be great having you back on the job."

Ted shook his head. "Hand me a beer."

## Chapter Six

After driving back to West Virginia with all his possessions—nine boxes, a bulky abs buster machine, and a worn out mattress set—Ted helped unload everything into a storage unit owned by Earl's brother. The evening wind gusted around them, scattering desiccated leaves across the service station's vacant lot.

"I appreciate your help, Earl," Ted said, placing a small box on a nearby stack. "Especially taking the time to stop by the factory for my final paycheck."

"Ain't no big thing."

"Well, it is to me."

"I'm just happy to be away from the house," Earl said, following Ted outside. "Kim honeydo's me to death on my off days."

"She is a bossy little fuss, isn't she?"

Earl grinned. "You know, you're more than welcome to store this stuff at our house."

"I appreciate your offer, but I think it's best to keep this stuff out of everyone's way." Ted pulled the storage door closed and caught glimpse of the *help wanted* sign next door in the service station's window. "Gary looking to hire somebody?"

"Yeah, his mechanic left him high and dry about a week ago. Doesn't pay much but it's a job, I guess."

Ted wiped his palms on his jeans. "I haven't seen

Gary since high school. How's he doing?"

"He's fine. Stays busy."

"I'm surprised he even speaks to you nowadays," Ted said. "Especially after all the teasing you gave him when we were kids over his stuttering problem."

"That's true. But he doesn't stutter near as much as he used to."

"Really?"

"Yeah, he learned he could control it some by sayin' *huh* at the beginning of difficult sentences."

"No kidding?"

"But he's the same old Gary. . . always workin'."

Ted secured the padlock before returning his attention to the sign. "I think I'll stop by and see him tomorrow."

"Whatever floats your boat, man." Earl dug the wad of snuff out of his gum line and flicked it across the pavement. "But you know you can make a lot more money in the mines."

"Yeah, but Myrtle won't beat me senseless for being a grease monkey."

Ted bounded the front porch steps upon reaching Myrtle's house.

The front door opened with Kim stepping out to greet him. "She fell asleep about an hour ago," she said, closing the door behind her.

"She eat anything?"

"A little bit of grilled chicken, not much though. She just doesn't seem to have an appetite."

"Doc Hamilton said we could expect that."

Kim glanced toward the driveway. "I'd best get going, Earl looks tired."

"Yeah, you might have to put some ice on his drinking arm."

"Oh, Lord, he hasn't done anything stupid, has he?"

"Depends on what you consider stupid." He held off grinning as long as he could. "I'm just messin' with you. He was fine."

"Lord, have mercy." She placed a hand on her forehead. "Are you trying to give me a heart attack?"

"Sorry, I couldn't resist. Thanks again for keeping an eye on things."

"Anytime." She kissed him on the cheek before heading down the steps. "I'll check on you two tomorrow."

The living room door creaked as Ted stepped inside. He waited until Kim safely made her way to the truck, where a glow highlighted Earl's face, the obvious draw of a cigarette. Smoke tendrils escaped the truck's cab when Kim opened the passenger door.

Ted quietly removed his boots and listened for possible stirrings from Myrtle's bedroom. Silence rang in his ears until the crunching gravel under tires drew his attention back to the driveway where Earl's truck was easing down the hollow, headlights fading with the engine whir.

"Is that you, Teddy?" Myrtle's voice was phlegmy, thin.

"Yes, ma'am." The sweet, chalky scent in her bedroom seemed to get heavier with time. "We just made it home."

Myrtle motioned for him to come closer. "Sit a spell."

He slid into the bedside chair.

"I just feel terrible that you're taking so much time off from work because of me." She licked her lips. "Don't get me wrong, I love having you here, but if you're not careful, you'll end up losin' your job."

"I left the factory, Gran. Picked up my final paycheck today."

She closed her eyes. "Call them first thing in the morning, you can't afford—"

"Listen, I'll get a job in town. . . at least until you get better."

Her eyebrows rimpled into the bridge of her nose. "Get better?" Her soft laughter spurred a coughing spat. She pressed a hand against her chest and breathed deeply. "Am I the *only* person around here that knows I'm dying?"

Ted stared in silence, watching the color slowly return to her cheeks.

"Wait a minute." She struggled to sit up. "What do you mean you'll get a *job* in town?"

"I'm going to talk with Earl's brother tomorrow about the mechanic position at the service station."

Her gaze narrowed. "You better not be lying to me."

"Seriously." He rubbed his neck. "I'm not going back to the mines."

"You better not. You made a promise."

"I know—"

"That coal mine is nothing more than a gateway to hell." She looked off to a blank space on the wall. "The lucky ones—Jeff and others like him—die before the real tragedy comes." Tears appeared at the corners of her reddening eyes. "I watched your granddaddy suffer for years as the mine took a little bit away from him every day—consuming him—from the inside out. And do I have to remind you what it did to him physically?" Her clenched fists trembled. "Do I?"

She jerked her hand away when Ted reached for it. "Don't look at me like I'm crazy, I know what I'm talking about!" The tears spilled onto her cheeks, streaming to her chin. "It ate away at his pride, his dignity. . ." Her voice quavered, softened. "His very soul."

Ted stared at the floor. He didn't know what to say. . . wasn't sure he would even be able to get it out if he did. And besides, when Myrtle's mind was made up, there was no talking her into or out of anything.

"I'm sorry, Teddy." Her voice was softer, raspy.

He gawked at her without speaking.

She touched his hand and stared out the window. "Have you ever noticed how coal dust makes a man look as though he's frowning?"

"What?"

"There's something about coal dust on a man's face that makes him look sad even when he's smiling." She wiped tears from her chin. "You know, like a mask."

"You don't have to worry, I'm not going back to the mines." He held back a sob, pushing against it, willing it to remain unsurfaced. "I promise."

Placing a stained coffee mug on the lowered tailgate of his

41

truck, Ted rummaged through the toolbox. Sunlight burned through the misty fog, bringing a false warmth to the November chill.

He found the hammer and crowbar near the bottom, just under the clutter of pipe wrenches, screwdrivers, and a thousand other items he hadn't thought about in ages. The cold steel felt natural in his hand, soothing.

*Have you ever noticed how coal dust makes a man look as though he's frowning?* Myrtle's words forced his thoughts toward his last moments with Jeff. They'd been working in the same section just before the explosion separated them.

He remembered the earth rumbling and creaking around them that day as they descended into the murky depths.

Jeff's soot face had camouflaged him against the darkness. "She's noisier than usual today," he'd said upon reaching their section.

Ted had stopped a moment to adjust his gear. "I need to head over to section six for a minute. You wanna go?"

"No, I'd better get started on the belt. Why are you going to six?"

"I need to see if Hank will let me off Saturday so I can take Lina shopping for a wedding gown."

"Wedding gown?" From his expression, it appeared as though a foul odor had accosted him. "It'll be more than a year before the two of you walk down the aisle."

"I know, but Lina wants to get the dress now."

Jeff nodded. "Of course she does."

"What's that supposed to mean?"

"It's down payment."

"No, I'm paying for the gown upfront."

"No, Doofus, the dress *is* the down payment." Jeff's teeth gleamed from his blackened face like cheap pearls. "It's insurance against you getting cold feet."

"This is the reason you're still single. You overanalyze everything."

Jeff grinned. "You're probably right about that, but you're going to need a boat load of luck to pull this one off."

"What are you talking about?"

"That girl is going to have you jumping through hoops before the wedding day ever gets here." He grinned again. "But those are hoops you're willing to jump through, and that says somethin'."

"That's what you do when you're in love, Jeff."

Jeff shook his head. "Here," he said, pulling something from his pocket. "I want you to have this." The worn coin had a tiny square cut from its center.

"You're lucky script? But, your dad gave it to you."

"It was a reminder for me to never wait for something I could already afford." He flipped the coin over in his palm. "This was worth fifty dollars at the Amherst Coal Company Store when it was still in operation." He held it up between forefinger and thumb. "Know what it's worth today?"

Ted shrugged.

"Not a dime." He laughed. "Fifty dollars was a lot of money back then, and Momma and Daddy sure could have used that money, but decided to hold on to it for hard times, which is not a bad idea. But when the company store closed, the script became a worthless piece of metal." His smile returned. "So when he gave this to me, he said to always plan for tomorrow but live for today."

He placed the coin in Ted's hand. "I think you can benefit from that advice yourself."

"I don't know what to say." Ted rubbed his thumb over the coin's face. "Thanks."

Jeff spit out a glob of tobacco and wiped his lips. "You'd better get going before someone puts Hank in a foul mood."

An odd rustling from the hillside pulled Ted from his memories, causing him to nearly drop the crowbar. The startling jolt coursed his nervous system like electricity. He scrutinized the hillside until he found a herd of deer grazing near the tree line.

"Sweet thunder," he said, pressing a hand against his chest. "Take it easy."

A brawny buck rose its impressively antlered head just seconds before the herd stampeded toward the ridge, the flood of hooves fulminating against the mountains.

He searched his pocket, finding the familiar coin. The polished face glimmered in the sunlight, reflecting over the truck bed.

Ted returned the coin to his pocket, secured the toolbox, and collected the gear. The section of wall he planned to dismantle appeared to be one massive piece of granite with grooves chiseled into it to simulate grout seams. But varying shades suggested the stones were individually mortared.

Pausing in front of Myrtle's window, Ted brushed dirt off the crowbar. Myrtle's frail form was curled up in her bed, the rising and falling of her chest the only signs of life. He remembered the fire in her eyes the night before and made his way to the wall. He wasn't quite sure what was harder to witness, her outburst or apologies.

A curt breeze forced him to button his jacket, the chill burning his cheeks and ears. Using the crowbar like a chisel, Ted guided the flattened end to a grout seam and brought the hammer down on the other end several times. The impact reverberated into his hand, stinging his fingers. Studying the unfazed surface, he sighed. *This is going to take longer than I'd thought.*

He glanced back at Myrtle's window. *Maybe I should wait until she's awake.* His wind-whipped pant legs stung his flesh as he collected the tools.

The storage building seemed to be nothing more than flimsy metal and cinderblocks. Ted climbed out of his truck and walked past. *Nine boxes.* After all these years his entire life was easily packed away in such a small space. He stepped inside the service station's waiting area and heard an impact wrench from the garage. "Hello?"

He scrunched his nose at the sulfur and headed for the bay area where he found Gary placing a wheel on a raised '85 Firebird.

Just a year older than Ted, Gary looked to be at least ten years his senior. The fingers of his combover clung to his scalp as if shellacked there, drawing more attention to his baldness than hiding it.

"You look a little busy," Ted said, trying not to startle the wiry man.

Gary turned, smiled. "Huh-How are ya, Ted?"

"Just fine." He nodded toward the racked car. "That yours?"

It looked as though Gary was trying to keep something from escaping his mouth. "Huh-Belongs to some kid from Crawley Creek."

"So, what's wrong with it?"

"I'm not sure—other than it smells like hellfire and brimstone."

"Have you checked the differential housing?"

Gary's expression glazed over.

Leaning under the car, Ted checked out the chassis. "That smell is a dead giveaway," he said, touching a dark spot near the front end and brought the viscous, oily muck to his nose. "There's your problem." He held his finger out for Gary to see. "Looks like the transfer case seal is cracked."

"Yeah?"

"Let me guess, the owner noticed the smell after a long trip?"

"Huh-He'd just got home from Myrtle Beach."

"It's not that big of a deal to fix," Ted said, wiping his hands with a service rag. "You just want to make sure you get all the old seal scraped off before installing the new one or you'll end up with a worse leak than this one."

"I didn't know you were a mechanic."

"I'm not." Ted grinned. "But all the junkers I've owned over the years have pretty much forced me into becoming a shade tree mechanic just to keep them on the road."

"Huh-How long are you planning to be in town?"

"Not sure. Myrtle's health is pretty poor. I came home to look after her." He rubbed his forehead, drawing a deep breath. "That's why I came to see you, actually. I wanted to ask about the job opening."

Gary grinned again. "Huh-When can you start?"

"How about right now?" Ted pulled his jacket off and rolled up his shirt sleeves. "By the way, how much does it pay?"

## Chapter Seven

A full moon peeked through bruise-colored clouds, highlighting the mountaintops as Ted left the service station, muscles burning from the wrench work. He didn't mind the exertion but the damp shirt sticking to his torso was another story. *What a day.*

He climbed inside the truck cab and cranked the ignition, flinching at the sudden blasting radio. Quickly lowering the volume, he breathed deeply before finally putting the gearshift into reverse.

The two-lane road cut through mountains and coal camps, every now and then tapering to a one-lane route. The headlight beams washed over wooded hillsides, occasionally reflecting in deer eyes like cheap flash photography. Ted lifted his foot from the gas pedal when Dorothy's Park 'N Eat came into view. It'd been years since he'd eaten there, yet found himself turning onto the parking lot.

Other than a few missing shingles, the building looked exactly as he remembered it. Mold pocked the white cinderblock exterior, growing most densely nearest the ground. He climbed out of the truck, staring at the lifeless neon sign until movement from the front entrance attracted his attention. Stepping closer, he discovered a Lost Dog flyer taped to the door, its bottom half flapping in the wind.

The muffled audio from the television inside grew louder as he opened the door. The patrons—a few elderly men drinking coffee—paid him no mind when he seated himself at the table nearest the door.

The televised game was a bit loud. Marshall University's offense was on the field, lined up against a crimson-uniformed team—all the green and red resembled a Christmas parade gone terribly awry.

"What can I get you to drink, hon?" A smiling waitress held out a menu for Ted.

"I'll take a Coke."

She pointed her pen at Ted. "Aren't you Myrtle's son?"

"Grandson."

"I'm sorry," she said, laughing. "I'm Lauren Maynard. We went to church together. . . a long time ago."

"I remember, my friend Jeff had a crush on you."

"Are you serious?"

"Yeah, he talked about you all the time."

She shook her head. "He never gave me a clue."

"That's just the way he was." Ted scanned the list of desserts on the chalkboard by the kitchen door. "What's today's special?"

"Salmon patties, pinto beans, and cornbread."

"Sounds good to me. And I'll take an order of the same to go, please."

"No problem. I'll be right back with your Coke."

Framed high school football jerseys covered the back wall—a blue and gold one from the Logan Wildcats, an orange and black one from the Chapmanville Tigers, and a blue and white one from the Man Hillbillies. Trophies, ribbons, and photos surrounded the jerseys, along with scribbled notes and signs.

"We just added a bunch of pictures a few days ago," the waitress said, placing the soft drink in front of him. "Maybe thirty or so."

"Where do you guys get all that stuff?"

"Parents mostly, and grandparents of students." Enthusiasm grew in her eyes. "Or former players reliving glory days."

"I don't remember ever seeing it, but then again, it's been several years since I've been here."

"We started the Spirit Wall about two years ago." She rolled her eyes when the front counter phone rang. "I'll be right back."

A particular photograph below the Logan jersey looked familiar. He squinted, trying to unblur silhouettes in the image.

He made his way to the back wall, keeping his focus on that specific still.

The shot captured a classic moment just after he and his teammates had won the regional Pigskin Championship during his senior year. A younger version of himself stared back from the photo, holding up a forefinger in front of him, signifying his team was number one.

Jeff stood next to him in the shot—his grin beamed through the muddy face-mask, making Ted nearly laugh out loud right there in the restaurant. A couple of days before the game, Jeff had toyed with the thoughts of joining the Marines, but Ted had talked him out of it, reasoning the potential dangers.

Ted's stomach roiled as his imagination morphed Jeff's football helmet into a miner's hardhat with attached light fixture. *I'm sorry, Jeff.*

"There you are," the waitress said, carrying a tray of food. Ted had no idea how long he'd been staring at the display.

"I don't mean to trouble you, but could I get both of those orders to go, please?"

"Sure thing. Just give me a second."

Lingering near the table, he purposely stared at the front door. The television's audio erupted in white noise, the football game disintegrating into gray pixels, crawling like hive bees.

One of the old men yelled something unintelligible at the screen, his face contorted, red. "Careful, Lionel," his friend said, chuckling. "You're 'bout to have a stroke."

Color flickered on the screen before the picture returned, revealing The Thundering Herd's quarterback lying on the field, obviously sacked at his own ten-yard line.

Ted cleared his throat, warmth entering his cheeks. *Come on, what's taking so long?*

The truck cab carried the scent of pattied salmon, reminding Ted of his childhood weekends where Myrtle cooked salmon cakes almost every Saturday—only she used mackerel in the place of salmon because it was cheaper. He gripped the steering wheel, forefingers drumming to a tune from the radio so familiar he couldn't quite identify the song or the artist.

In spite of the bright moonlight, darkness crowded the headlight beams where Ted's gaze fixed on the blurring road. He smiled at the thought of Myrtle's excitement once she'd learn what he'd picked up for supper. Anything to see the twinkle in her eyes again.

He slowed at the first glimpse of the steep curve ahead, laboring the steering wheel with his left hand, steadying the food containers in the passenger seat with his right. He jerked the wheel, swerving the truck toward the shoulder when an enormous shadow swam across the windshield.

Leaning forward, he scanned the treetops before shutting off the static-stricken radio and shifted his gaze through the side window.

The thoughts of Duke surprised him. He'd hated how the rooster had attacked him every time he gathered eggs. He remembered standing outside the henhouse door for seemingly hours, empty cartons in hand, dread fouling his stomach.

An eerie hush came over the truck cab, the roadside chorus of frogs and crickets disappearing with it. He scanned the darkness, squinting. Thunderless lightening flashed in the distance, briefly revealing something flying in his side- and rearview mirrors. "What was that?"

The truck rocked with a crashing impact from above. Ted started at the scratching and scrambling from the cab's roof. Maybe a black bear had leaped from some mountainous ledge and was now trying to maul its way inside. It was a ridiculous thought, he knew, but what else could it be? He squeezed his knees together, pushing back bladder pressure.

Flooring the gas pedal, he continued searching for a glimpse of whatever was on the roof. His heart pummeled his chest, pounding in his ears. He knew it would be a stupid thing to do, but he considered cracking the window a bit just before a screech set his skin crawling with goose pimples. *That's no bear.*

A dark, veiny membrane briefly draped over the windshield, obscuring his view of the road before disappearing overhead again. Something in the air caused him to recall the scent from the cracked transfer case seal he'd worked on all day. The second the thought crossed his mind, he practically stood on the brake pedal, causing the truck's stopping force to press his body into the activated seatbelt.

The roof warped overhead, groaning with obvious weight. As if by instinct, he punched the gas pedal again, swerving the truck from side to side, while oscillating his gaze from road to rearview mirror.

The overhead commotion ceased a split-second before something hit the tailgate, knocking it to its lowered position. Ted checked the rearview mirror and found a man-like silhouette rolling a few times on the pavement before rising to a standing position.

Just before heading into a steep curve, a pair of crimson orbs glowing where the creature's eyes should be caught his attention. He adjusted the rearview mirror when he saw what he thought were enormous wings unfurling from the thing's outline.

Ted maintained his attention to the mirror even after driving into the curve, praying whatever he'd seen would not follow him. Slowing the truck to a near crawl for safety, he wiped perspiration from his eyes. Then he saw glowing red coming around the bend in the distance behind him. He blinked hard, rubbed his irritated sockets. The red began flashing the closer it approached, then mixing with blue, revealing the strobing lights of a police cruiser.

"Great," he said, pulling to the side of the road.

He put the truck in park and pulled his driver's license out of his wallet. After what felt like the longest moments of his life, he watched a figure emerge from the cruiser, adjusting an enormous Smokey Bear hat, while walking toward the truck.

Probably saw me swerving all over the place.

"License and registration, please," the officer said from behind his flashlight's glare.

Ted handed the license to him and started collecting the other items from the sun visor.

The officer directed the light into Ted's face after momentarily scanning the license. "Well, if it isn't Ted Browning."

Ted squinted past the light and barely read the name badge on the uniform: SHERIFF ADAMS. "Hello, Mark." The sudden dryness in his mouth caused him to annunciate each word slowly, deliberately. "Myrtle told me you'd been elected—"

"What are you doing here?" Adams said, moving the light and his attention back to the driving documents. "I

54

thought you'd moved out of state. . . for good."

"Well, I moved—"

"Do you know why I pulled you over?"

Ted paused, studying the man's face. "Not really."

"You were doing 25 miles an hour in a 55 zone." He moved the light back into Ted's face. "How much have you had to drink?"

"Excuse me?"

"I see this all the time," he said, leaning so close Ted could see the fraying end of the toothpick in the corner of his mouth. "It's weird how most drunks think they're driving normal but they're actually creeping along like a ninety-year-old."

"I haven't been drinking."

He smirked. "Would you be willing to take a breathalyzer?"

"I sure would, if that's what it takes. But I assure you I have not been drinking."

"Well then." Adams quietly stared into Ted's face, obviously reading every nuance. "If you haven't been drinking, then why were you driving so slowly?"

Ted glanced into the rearview mirror. "Well, I saw a few deer close to the road. I was afraid one was going to bolt out in front of the truck."

Adams squinted, his gaze never straying from Ted's face. "Deer, huh?"

"I hit one several years ago—totaled my old truck. You would have thought I'd collided with a tank."

Adams raised an eyebrow, his gaze still fixed on Ted's face. The cadence of crickets was nearly hypnotic, soothing. "All right," he finally said, returning the identification. "Have a safe trip back out of state."

Ted waited for him to drive away before starting the truck. He scanned the skies as he pulled onto the road, heading toward Coal Branch Hollow.

Ted collected the food containers and locked the driver's-side door. The cool night air nipped at his ears, prompting him to climb the porch steps two at a time.

He removed his boots and tiptoed toward the kitchen, pausing at the sight of something in the hall in front of Myrtle's room. The darkness made identifying the object difficult, but as best as he could tell, it was a good-sized lump low to the floor.

He eased toward the wall, staring into the shadows, while keeping a cautious eye on the mass. When his fingers reached the light switch, he paused, trying to formulate some plan for whatever might happen. He set his feet into a wide stance, took a deep breath, and flipped the switch.

A burning—very much like a reversing whiskey trail—bloomed in his chest, surging into his throat at the sight of Myrtle lying face down, lifeless.

"Gran?" He dropped to his knees, turning her over. "Gran, can you hear me?"

The faint rising and falling of her chest did little to extinguish the flame now in his throat. Gently picking her up, he carried her to the bedroom where he found pillows and blankets strewn across the floor. He placed her into the bed, pulled the covers to her shoulders, and searched the nightstand. *Where's the telephone?*

He recognized the scent of dirt, which caused him to briefly scan the room for an explanation. He put a hand on her shoulder. "Gran?" Her eyelids fluttered. "Are you okay?"

"What. . . " Her gaze seemed to register that someone was next to the bed. "Noooo! I told you to leave me alone!" She pushed back, kicking at the blankets, nearly falling out of the bed. "Please, Jesus! Help me!"

Ted grabbed her wrists. "Gran, it's—"

"Let me go, you. . . " She braced a foot against his chest and pushed back, pulling her arms, working to break free of his grip. ". . . evil thing!"

"Gran, it's me!" Her strength was surprisingly good, especially for an aging woman with only a few months to live. "It's me, Ted!"

Her expression gradually softened, tears pooling in her eyes. "Teddy. . . " Deep sobs shook her body as she covered her face with trembling hands. She tried to speak again but gave up when the sobs turned to whimpers. A wail emerged from her, steadily increasing as she rocked back and forth.

"It's okay." He put an arm around her back as he slid next to her. "Everything's okay." Dried blood made the scratches on her arms appear larger and worse than they really were.

Her wails fell into staccato sobs as she pressed her head into his collarbone.

The strongest person he ever knew—the woman who once shooed a bear out of the rose garden with a broom—broken. Something grew in his throat. "I'm here," he whispered. They were the same consoling words she'd whispered a thousand times to him over the years.

He stroked her wiry hair. "Are you okay?"

"Where'd it go?" Her voice was thin, furtive.

"Where did *what* go?"

She searched the room. "That. . . thing!"

Ted drew his head back, pushing his eyebrows down. "Just relax, there's nothing here but the two of us."

"It was the devil!"

He stared at her for a moment. "What?"

"The devil." She craned her neck, focusing her gaze on the doorway behind him. "Or some demon straight from the pits of hell!"

"The doctor told you the medicine would—"

"I know what I saw, Teddy! It was *here*, I tell you!" An awkward silence came over the room as she wiped her eyes. "Smelled like damnation."

He gently squeezed her arm. "It's gone now."

"I see," she said, pulling her arm away. "You don't believe me, do you? You think the old woman is too doped up to even know what she's talking about, huh?"

"All I'm saying is that whatever you saw is now obviously gone."

She leaned back into her pillows, stared out the window. "It stood at the foot of the bed, glaring down at me like it was the grim reaper, waitin' for me to cross chilly Jordan. . . Lord, if I could get those red eyes out my mind."

Ted leaned forward. "What did you say?"

She turned her attention back to him. "I said it stood

right there at the foot of the bed."

"No, what about its eyes?"

"They was glowin' red." She stole a glance at the doorway behind him again. "Something came over me. . . like I was sick or somethin'. . . but I wasn't sick. It was like somethin' inside me knew that thing was. . . wrong. . . or. . . pure evil."

He brushed a strand of hair out of her eyes. "Try to get some sleep, I'll be in the next room if you need me." He picked up an empty plate from the nightstand.

"Teddy?" She waited until he was looking at her. "When I'm gone, I want you to get out of this town, you hear me?"

He tried to smile. "Good night, Gran."

The cold linoleum bit his feet through the thin socks, making him wonder if he'd forgotten to set the thermostat before leaving for work. Placing the dish in the kitchen sink, he noticed the back door curtains moving. Stepping closer, he found the door ajar, a gentle breeze brushing past him.

He glanced back toward Myrtle's room and closed the door.

## Chapter Eight

Ted found Gary sweeping out the bays when he got to work the next morning. Sunlight poked through the windows, revealing fog outside.

"Mornin'," Ted said, handing a cup of coffee to him.

"Huh-Thank you."

"You might want to take a drink before you thank me." Ted grinned. "I bought it at Speedlane, and I'm pretty sure it's made from tires that can no longer be re-tread."

Gary sipped from the cup, grimaced. "I see what you mean, it's a little. . . huh *flat*, isn't it?"

Ted chuckled. "What time did you get out of here last night?"

"Huh-Left around eleven-thirty."

"What in the world keeps you here so late?"

"Day-to-day things I don't have time to get done during regular hours."

Ted held his cup to his lips. "Sounds exciting."

"Huh-Yeah, very boring. Had some excitement a few nights ago, though." He swept up the debris and brushed it into a garbage can. "It's usually as quiet as the liquor store on Sunday here, but there was a racket out back that would have raised the dead."

"What was it?"

"I'm not sure, but the back door window was broke.

. . cut my finger cleaning up the glass before getting it replaced." He held up a bandaged finger. "At first I thought it was some guy getting high or trying to break into the garage." He bowed his head, rubbing his eyes. "By the time I came inside to get my 9mm and returned, he. . . or whatever it was, was gone."

"Whatever *it* was?"

"Huh-Yeah," he said, motioning for Ted to follow him. "I couldn't see very clearly because of the telephone pole it was behind." They walked out the back door and down the alley. "There," he said, pointing at a particular area. "Huh-that's where it was." He stopped walking and stared at the location as if waiting for something to happen.

"Are you okay?"

Gary didn't move. "It felt. . . *bad*." His gaze never left the area. "It's hard to explain, but it felt. . . *odd*." He shook his head. "Huh-that's still not the right word."

Ted stared at the telephone pole.

"The next morning I came back out here to look around." He walked closer to the area. "I figured I would find beer cans, needles, or something like that. I was surprised to find this." He pointed at the ground directly behind the pole.

Ted stepped closer and saw that the grass and weeds were dead, black dead, as if someone had poured toxic waste on the area. "What in the world is this?" His gaze followed the dead trail to its starting point, about six feet from the pole. "I've never seen anything like this."

"Huh-me either."

Ted squatted, getting a better look. The grass and weeds did not appear to be covered by chemicals.

"Huh-evil."

Ted looked up at Gary. "What?"

"Huh-that's the word." Gary's gaze followed the dead trail to its abrupt end. "It felt *evil.*"

Ted rose, avoiding eye contact.

"I know that sounds weird, but that's exactly what I felt. It was so bad I thought I was going to throw up."

A cold breeze whistled around them.

"That's not all."

Ted felt for his cigarettes. "What do you mean?"

"There was a dog there."

"A *dog*?"

"Huh-it was dead, torn up pretty bad." He closed his eyes for a few seconds. "But, it was gone the next morning. Huh-not a trace."

"Did you report this to the police?"

He shook his head. "I was afraid they'd think I was on drugs or something."

Ted lit a Marlboro, drawing the smoke into his lungs and releasing it through his nostrils. "You think the thing was eating the dog?"

"Huh-not sure, but the poor thing was mutilated nearly beyond recognition." He rubbed his forehead. "You probably think I'm crazy, but I'm telling you the truth."

"No, I believe you." Ted nodded. "I don't want to believe you, but I do."

Ted was surprised to find Myrtle awake when he returned

home from work that evening. She had the bed raised and was sitting up reading her Bible.

"You look as though you're feeling better," he said, stepping into her bedroom.

"I feel pretty good."

"I'm sure glad." He sank into the chair next to the bed. "You gave me an awful scare last night."

She puckered her chin. "I'm sorry, Teddy." She reached for his hand. "But, I want you to remember what I told you about getting out of this town when I'm gone."

"Let's not talk about—"

"Listen to me." She leaned close to him, putting both hands on his. "I'm ready to go. I'm tired of waiting." She leaned back into the bed, closed the Bible. "It reminds me of the time I took a train to Roanoke to visit my Aunt Emma when I was just a young girl. She'd been sick and needed someone to help her around the house for a few months."

"I never knew you'd been outside of West Virginia."

"Well, to be honest, I didn't think I'd ever make it back." Her eyebrows moved up her forehead. "The longest day of my life was spent sitting in that Roanoke train station waiting to get home."

She stared out the window, her gaze fixed on something from the past. "The depot man kept sayin' the train was due any time, but the minutes eventually crawled to hours. And I waited. I listened for the whistle. I anticipated the rumble. I fell asleep a few times, and then waited some more." She smiled. "Just when I thought the train wasn't coming, I heard the whistle echoing from afar."

The uncomfortable pause crept into Ted's bones. He watched her face, giving her time to finish speaking.

"I can hear that distant whistle right now, Teddy." Her gaze finally met his. "Why don't you sing to me like you did when you was a boy?"

"Come on," he said, shaking his head. "You know I haven't sung in years."

She took his hand. "Everyone at church always bragged that you had the most beautiful voice. And nobody could sing 'Life's Railway to Heaven' like you could. Do you remember that song?"

"Vaguely."

"Sing it for me, Teddy." Her eyes all but sparkled. "Sing it real slow like you always did in church."

The eagerness in her eyes was more than he could take. The words came back to him as though they were alive in his head. Her eyes closed in sleep sometime during the second verse. He sang the chorus again before rising to his feet.

Picking up the oatmeal bowl from the nightstand, he quietly headed for the kitchen. The tune from the old hymn still lingered with him, reminding him of Myrtle's smile when he sang.

Placing the bowl in the kitchen sink, he noticed something in the yard while gazing out the window. He leaned forward, squinting for a better look.

He opened the back door and found dead black grass at the doorstep, leading a dark trail about twenty feet into the clearing where it abruptly ended.

## Chapter Nine

Ted brought the hammer down on the chisel again and realized he hadn't even scratched the wall's grout line with the past five strokes. Recoiling metal stung his hand as he raised the hammer and brought it down with the same fruitless result.

Movement in his peripheral vision caught his attention. He immediately noticed Myrtle through her window, sitting up in the hospital bed. *There must be more I can do for her.*

She met Ted's gaze, smiled. It was a good smile. One he hadn't seen from her in quite some time. He also noticed the warm color in her cheeks and smiled back at her.

Angling the chisel forty-five degrees over the mortar bead, he brought the hammer down on it. This time a small, granite-like chip broke away, resembling the ancient arrowhead he and Jeff had found in the mountains when they were in the boy scouts. He positioned the chisel's blade directly into the center of the freshly-notched area and hammered into it. Searching for a sign of progress, he found no cracks. No breaks. Not even a scratch.

He glanced back at Myrtle and found her grinning broadly at him—or as she would have put it, 'grinnin' like a possum eatin' sand-briars.' He shrugged. "What?"

She pointed at the stone wall. "I told you it was going to be a tough job." Her voice was faint from the other side of the window. "But you wouldn't listen to me."

He held up the grout fragment. "I'm getting there, just give me time."

She returned her attention to her Bible, still chuckling.

Ted frowned at his watch when he realized he had mere minutes to get to work. Gathering all the tools, he glanced again at Myrtle before heading for his truck.

Ted pushed the drain catch under the racked F-150's oil pan and removed the truck's plug. A dark stream glunked into the top pan, slowly abating. He noticed brake dust residue dulling one of the chrome rims, prompting him to get a better look.

The impact wrench jerked in his hands until the stubborn lug nuts twisted off one by one. The draining oil was now a thread-thin stream. Pulling the wheel from the axle and easing it to the floor, he shook his head at the worn-into-metal brake pad and rotor. *This is turning into a bigger job than I'd expected.*

The bell over the front door jingled from the office, reminding him Gary had stepped out for lunch. "I'll be right with you," he said, projecting his voice. He wiped his hands on a faded rag, touched the Marlboro pack in his shirt pocket, and entered the office.

"Can I help. . . "

"Ted?" Lina stepped forward, her eyes taking inventory of him. "Is that you?"

His legs seemed waterlogged—heavy, weak. "Hey there," he said, brushing grit from his shirt. "How have you been?"

"Oh, my gosh, I had no idea you were back in West Virginia." Her smile reminded him of the day he'd proposed to her. He even thought he could smell the baking pizzas from that night in the corner booth of Giovanni's when he surprised her with the ring. "You haven't changed a bit."

He cleared his throat. "Neither have you." He hoped she didn't notice his flushing cheeks.

"How's Myrtle?"

"Not too good, actually." He swallowed hard. "She has terminal cancer."

Tears reddened her eyes. "Is she doing all right?"

Ted thought she was moving to hug him, but relaxed when she fished a tissue out of her purse. "She's weak and doesn't have much of an appetite." He tried to smile. "But she amazes me with her positive outlook."

Lina laughed. "That doesn't surprise me. She's an amazing woman."

He shifted feet after not moving for what seemed an eternity. "I saw Mark last night." He tried to swallow back the lump in his throat. "I guess being the Sheriff's wife keeps you out of speeding tickets."

She laughed. "Well, we've been separated for about six months, so I have to watch my speed now more than ever."

"I'm sorry, I didn't know."

"Oh, it's fine." She shook her head. "The divorce will be final in a few weeks. And it can't come soon enough for me."

"So, what are you doing now?"

"Well, I went back to school about five years ago, and that's actually when the problems began. Mark thought he owned me, thought I was supposed to just give up my life and do whatever he said, and he hated the idea of me finishing my education." She rolled her eyes. "He's such a control freak. So, now I'm a registered nurse, working at the hospital."

"Good for you." Her smile returned, warming something inside him. "Look," he said, scratching an eyebrow. "I wanted to apologize for—"

"That's not necessary." She dabbed at her eyes with a tissue. "Although, I'm not gonna lie, I was devastated at first." Her voice quavered. "But I got a small glimpse at what you've been through when Mom passed away." A tear crept down her cheek. "I realize I was more selfish than anything, but I knew deep down you had to leave. I mean, losing your parents at such an early age, then your best friend. . . " She closed her eyes. "And then carrying the feelings of guilt must have been a tremendous weight."

Ted was glad she didn't use the phrase *survivor's guilt*. He'd heard that so often it made him sick. Yes, he was alive, yes, he felt guilt, but he was anything but a survivor. "So. . . " He rubbed the back of his neck. "What brings you in today?"

"Um. . . " She motioned toward the parking lot. "My check-engine light came on."

"Let's take a look," he said, walking toward the door.

He propped the Ford Fusion's hood with the metal

stand and touched the radiator cap. "When was the last time you had the oil changed?"

"About six weeks ago," she said, moving next to him.

A relentless wind swirled the same perfume she always wore—Sweet Honesty by Avon—about him, snatching his breath. "I'm sorry, what did you say?"

"Six weeks."

Using a soiled rag, he cautiously twisted the radiator cap, feeling for possible gurgling or pressure. When he was sure it was safe, he removed the cap. "That's the problem," he said, peering into the reservoir. "Your radiator fluid is low."

"Oh, thank God. I couldn't afford any major repairs right now."

"It's not a big deal at all." He placed a funnel in the reservoir and poured from a new container. "If it happens again, then we need to check if there is a leak in the radiator."

"It is so good to see you."

Ted smiled. "It was good seeing you, too."

Ted dumped Raisin Bran into what Myrtle jokingly referred to as Ted's *Jethro bowl*, hoping the noise from his late-night snack wouldn't awaken her. He smiled at the thought of her falling asleep—mid-sentence, mind you—while talking about not being sleepy. It then dawned on him that this could be an unfavorable sign Dr. Hamilton failed to warn him about.

He took the milk from the refrigerator, sniffed its contents, and placed it on the table. As he picked up the sugar canister from the countertop, he noticed a stack of letters stashed away behind it. He flipped though the pieces and realized they were bills from Logan Regional Medical Center.

Noting the absence of postage on the envelopes, he opened the first piece and scanned the information. "That sly fox." He glanced over his shoulder. *She brought these home from the hospital and hid them while I wasn't around.*

He slid into a chair, adding numbers in his head. The hospital stay was expensive, but the tests they'd administered were through the roof. He had no idea that cancer care would total over one hundred-thousand dollars. . . and that was after Medicaid paid its portion. *And she doesn't have insurance.*

He took in the kitchen—the cook stove where Myrtle had baked countless biscuits and pies and cornbread, the *Lord Bless This Mess* sign over the sink, and the backdoor's frame marked with growth measurements for him and Jeff when they were in middle school. *She's gonna have to sell the house to pay these bills.*

He rose from the table, returned the milk carton to the fridge, and poured the cereal back into its box. *What is she thinking?*

He punched in Kim's home phone number on Myrtle's cell phone as he made his way to the front door. A light breeze cooled his face as he stepped outside. After several rings, Kim's recorded voice invited callers to leave a message after the tone.

"Kim, this is Ted." He closed his eyes. "Tell Earl to let Jerry know I'd like to get back into the mines." Glancing toward the front door, he sighed. "I don't want Myrtle to know anything about this, so let's keep it between us, please. Thanks." He ended the call and reached for his smokes.

## Chapter Ten

Ted swung the sledgehammer again, focusing the impact on a particular stone at the top of the wall. Dust rose like smoke from newly formed mortar cracks. *Finally.* While moving the stone back and forth, he realized it was clinging to the wall like a deeply rooted tooth.

Placing both hands at the top, he curled his fingers over the top, and pulled, revealing the protruding cone shape at the bottom of the stone, which interlocked in a mortise-and-tenon fashion into the layer beneath it. *What on Earth?*

He lifted the stone straight up from the wall—not expecting its heft—as broken mortar tumbled into the coned mortise. He dropped the slab a few feet away, grimacing as it thunked to the ground.

The engine whir of what sounded to be a mid-sized car echoed up the hollow, drawing him to the corner of the house. He watched closely as a blue Ford Fusion pulled into the driveway, coming to a halt just behind his truck. He willed away a smile when Lina stepped out of the vehicle, waving at him.

"I'm sorry for dropping by unexpectedly like this," she said. "But I wanted to check on Myrtle. She's always been good to me. . . even after you and I were over."

"She always thought the world of you," Ted said, "And I'm sure she'd love to see you, but she's sleeping right now."

"So, you're hiding behind the house until she wakes up?" Lina said, chuckling.

He motioned for her to follow. "I'm opening up a section of the stone wall so Myrtle can see her roses."

"I helped her with the roses a few years." Lina's gaze made it to Myrtle's window where the frail woman slept in the shadows. She turned back to Ted, visibly shaken.

"I'll tell you one thing," he said, raising his eyebrows. "I've never dealt with a tougher mortar and stone combo than I have with this wall."

She grinned. "I can hear Myrtle bragging how, 'They don't make 'em like they used to.'"

"I'm beginning to believe her."

After a brief silence, she stared at her purse. "I was a little shocked to see you today."

"Sorry about that."

"I didn't mean it that way." Her cheeks reddened. "I just meant I wasn't expecting to see you."

"Well, to be honest, I wasn't expecting to see *you*, either."

She held her gaze to the extracted stone on the ground. "But, it got me to thinking about something that's been on my mind since you left." She reached into her purse and retrieved a black velvet ring box. "I want you to have this back."

"Why don't you just keep that?" He tugged at the teeshirt riding up his neck. "After what I put you through. . . "

"I'd rather you have it." She put the box in his hand,

closed his fingers around it. "Besides, I couldn't keep it knowing it was your momma's wedding ring." Her warm touch sent shivers through him.

"Thanks."

"You know," she said with a playful smile. "You told me you were going to take me to the beach."

"What?"

"A week before everything happened, you'd promised to take me to Myrtle Beach."

The ambery floral fragrance of her perfume drifted past him. "Well. . . I. . ."

"I was so excited about going to the beach, I couldn't focus on anything else." Her smile wavered. "All I could think about was digging my toes in the sand and letting the water wash over them."

"I'm so sorry."

"Don't be." Her smile returned. "I guess what I'm trying to say is it took a while for me to realize I wasn't ready for marriage—that I was too immature to be making a decision of that magnitude." She traced a finger over his jawline. "And the thing that brought it to my attention more than anything was coming to terms with the fact I was more angry at you for not taking me to the beach than I was at you for dumping me."

Ted cleared his throat. "We were young, that's for sure."

"So, I don't feel that you put me through anything." Her playful smile returned. "But I do blame you for the fact that I've never had the chance to stick my toes in the sand."

His laughter was full, eventually morphing into a sincere grin. "Thank you, Lina."

"No problem." She kicked at the stone on the ground. "Looks like you've got your hands full."

He glanced at Myrtle's slumbering figure. "You have no idea."

Ted handed Myrtle a spoon and a napkin. "Be careful, soup's a tad hot," he said. "Want me to fix you a peanut butter sandwich or something?"

"No, honey, I'm fine. Thank you, though."

Thunder rumbled over the house as a heavy rain pummeled the rooftop, sounding as though an enormous fan was running in the next room. Ted searched the ceiling, surprised to find no leaks.

"I hate this rain," Myrtle said, staring out the window.

"Your roses need it."

She shook her head. "Not *this* kind of rain. This is the lingering type of storm that causes flash flooding. The kind of rain that breaks stems and rips leaves." She coughed into a handkerchief. "The kind of rain that took your mom and dad from us."

"The Buffalo Creek flood." He realized he'd said it out loud and rubbed the back of his neck. "I was what, two?"

Myrtle nodded without looking at him. "Just a mere pup. That slurry pond sat at the head of Buffalo Creek without any problems until the rain came down like it's doing right now, and kept a comin'."

He put a spoonful of soup to his lips, blew.

"When the side of the pond broke, a wall of black water came through that hollow like a ragin' bull, destroyin' everything in sight." Her gaze fell to her hands. "You'd been sickly for right at a week or so and your momma asked me to watch you 'til they got back from visiting your uncle Denver."

The soup scalded Ted's tongue, urging a sip of water.

"I'll never forget that day." She turned toward him. "I'll never forget the phone call, either."

"I'm sure getting a call like that stays with you." Ted tried to smile. "It must have been terrifying to hear from the State Police during all the chaos."

She stared out the window again. "That ain't the call I'm talkin' about."

He waited for her to explain. Even thought for a moment that she was not going to say anything.

"I got a call about an hour before your parents left for Denver's house." Her trembling hands touched her cheeks. "There were a lot of noises on the line. . . some kind of electronic gibberish."

Ted cleared his throat.

"Naturally, I thought one of the neighbor's yungins was goofing around on the party line." Her face became ashen. "But when I heard that voice, I knowed it was somethin' serious."

Ted tried to put the call she'd received out of his mind.

"It wasn't really a voice," Myrtle said, leaning toward him. "They was more like wet whispers or, I don't know, just weird noises." Her smile bloomed across her face. "But I distinctly remember it sayin', 'The buffalo will drown.'" She raised her eyebrows. "And then that flood hit Buffalo Creek, drowning all them people."

He caressed her arm, worried that his attempt at smiling would come across as a grimace.

"Tell me the truth," she said, squeezing his hand. "Are you back working at the Bear Creek Mine?"

"Of course not," Ted said, trying to look offended. "Why would you ask?"

Her gaze was somewhere between a stare and a glare. "'Cause I got another call today—same noises, same weird voice—and this time it said, 'the bear would be crushed.'"

## Chapter Eleven

The folding chair creaked beneath Ted as he tried to get comfortable while filling out the employment application in the waiting area of the Bear Creek mine. Every time the chair squeaked with his movement, he glanced at the receptionist, but she never looked up from her own paperwork.

The side door opened, allowing a breeze to blast through the room, fluttering Ted's papers as two men walked in. Coal-dusted faces hid the identities of the men.

"Ted?" The tallest man's teeth gleamed through the grime. "Ted Browning, is that you?"

Ted stared into the man's eyes, searching for a clue. "Leo?"

"You're the last person I'd ever dreamed to see here." His smile revealed a wad of tobacco squirreled away in his jaw. "How've you been?"

There was comfort in the firm handshake. "Fine, just fine."

"It's been forever since I've laid eyes on you."

Ted nodded. "It's been twenty years."

"Lord, have mercy, has it been that long?"

A fella in his early twenties came up behind Leo, grinning. "Is this old geezer bothering you, sir?" He let out a shrill laugh, slapped Leo on the back. "We try an' keep him from botherin' normal folks, but he strays off every now and again."

Leo offered what looked to be an obligatory chuckle. "Jimmy, I want you to meet Ted Browning."

The young man's eyes widened. "Are you kidding me?" He shook Ted's hand like he was working the handle of an old fashioned water pump. "It sure is an honor to meet you."

Ted's cheek's tingled with warmth.

"Leo told me 'bout how you survived the disaster by digging through the debris with your bare hands." He glanced at the old man. "Then how you volunteered to go back to find your buddy when you found out he'd not made it out."

Leo slapped the young man in the back of the head. "That's enough, doofus, you're going to pump his arm right off his shoulder."

"Sorry, but I ain't never met a hero before."

"I'm no hero." Ted was surprised by the sharp tone of his voice, focused on softening it. "If I was a hero, Jeff would be alive today."

Leo squeezed Ted's shoulder. "The hero is a hero because of his courage to try—it has nothing to do with success or failure." His gaze moved to the application in Ted's hand. "So, you thinking about coming back?"

Happy for the digression, Ted nodded. "Yeah, I'm checking out all my options."

"Jerry know you're here?"

"He's supposed to be out in a minute."

"Just be careful if you get near section eleven," the young man said, leaning forward. "They's a lot a strange noises going' on around there." He stole a quick glance at the door before lowering his voice to a whisper. "And nobody can account for those noises."

"That's what I've heard. Weird noises, including what sounds like huge fluttering wings."

The young man pointed at Ted. "That's right! It's the Mothman. Some of the guys think he's nested hisself somewhere in section eleven."

Leo rolled his eyes. "All right, let's not get carried away." He grinned at Ted before returning his attention to the young man. "There's no such thing as a Mothman. Plus, there's plenty of things to fear down there without having to make up monsters and such."

"Coal mines have always produced the unexplained," Ted added. "Especially if you're claustrophobic or have issues with darkness."

Leo nodded. "If I told all of what I've seen or heard in my forty years underground, why they'd lock me in the looney bin." He shrugged. "You can't reason everything. All you can do is manage your job and keep going."

The young man cocked an eyebrow. "Well, what about the broken seal in section eleven? Can you explain that?"

Leo let out an exaggerated sigh. "Can't you see that some of the other men are doing things just so they can work easier sections?"

"So you think one of the miners. . . "

Ted followed the young man's distracted gaze, finding Jerry Price emerging from his office.

"Well, look what the cat drug in," Jerry said. "I heard

you were back in town." His smile was like a wool coat in January.

"It's good to see you, boss man."

Jerry ignored Ted's extended hand, hugging him. "It's good to see you, too." He held Ted back by the shoulders to get a good look. "You've grown up on us."

"Well, it's been twenty years."

Jerry let out a low whistle. "Where has the time gone?"

"Time flies when you're havin' fun," the young man said.

Leo slapped him in the back of the head. "Will you shut up?" He turned to Ted, then to Jerry. "We're gonna get out of here so you two can talk." He tugged at the young man's arm. "Let's go, motormouth."

"What did I do?"

"Just go."

Jerry took a chair beside Ted. "So, what brings you to Bear Creek?"

"I wanted to see if you have any openings."

Deep lines creased Jerry's forehead. "Does Myrtle know you're here?"

"What?" Ted cleared his throat. "I mean. . . no, she has no idea." He picked at a hangnail. "And I'd like to keep it that way if at all possible."

"We'll, that's not a problem." Jerry leaned back in the chair. "'Cause I sure don't want her ticked off at me."

"That's two of us."

"So, when can you start?"

"How about tonight?"

The service station's front door was locked, causing Ted to give the lone car in the parking lot a second look. He knew Gary was always in the building at least an hour before opening just to make sure everything was in order. *That's strange.* The ridges on the key were as sharp as briars, catching the cloth inside his pocket before unlocking the door.

"Gary?" He flipped the light switch, squinted at the overturned cash register.

Dark splotches speckled the floor with broken glass and paper. Flies circled the room as he started for the garage bays. *Is that transmission fluid?* He crouched over the debris, brushing a piece of paper through a particular splotch. *Blood.*

A rancid breeze scattered foliage into the office. "Gary? Are you here?"

The bay area was dark and stuffy, its floor littered with splotches and debris as well. The back door stood ajar, allowing a thin sliver of light to stretch across the floor. *Why would someone do this?*

The hairs on his arms rose when he noticed leaves settling against something on the ground just outside. A shoe? Cautiously pushing the door open, he listened for movement before stepping outside. The figure was a mess—lying face up, tatters of clothing clinging to mutilated flesh. Flies lifted from the gore when Ted stepped closer. He knelt beside the body and shooed the flies away. "Gary, can you hear me?"

The smell seemed to coat the back of his throat with a tinge of copper, gagging him. He pulled Myrtle's cell phone from his pocket and stared at the illuminated numbers as if they were foreign to him before punching in 9-1-1. He checked Gary's chest, watching for movement, finding none. "Yes, please send an ambulance to Gary's Garage on Main Street."

Switching the phone from one ear to the next, he noticed the yellowing weeds stretching from Gary's body toward the mountain. He realized a woman was speaking in the receiver, but wasn't sure what she was saying. "Just hurry. . . please!"

A hillside crash of branches and leaves sent him reeling backwards, dropping the phone. His gaze found something exiting the treetops, moving into the sky and out of sight. A glint of red was the last thing he saw through the darkening clouds.

## Chapter Twelve

Ted sat at the front counter, watching what appeared to be a platoon of deputies and State Troopers coming and going. In fact, officers had questioned him twice by the time Sheriff Adams made it to the scene.

The lanky lawman kept his gaze locked onto Ted's as he spoke to a few uniformed men near the door. "So," he said, walking toward the counter. "You wanna tell me what happened here?"

Ted shrugged. "No idea. This is how the place looked when I got here."

Adams crossed his arms over his chest. "Is that right?"

"I'd been working here for a few days and came in early today to let Gary know I was taking a job at Bear Creek."

"So, you're staying in town?"

"My grandmother has terminal cancer," Ted said. "I'm here to take care of her."

Adams pulled the mangled toothpick from his lips, pointed it toward the garage area. "What I want to know is what happened between you and Gary."

"What do you mean?"

"You know what I mean." He stared into Ted, squinting. "Did he get angry because you were leaving? Call you a few names? Did he throw the first punch?"

"Have you ever *met* Gary?"

"Don't get smart with me," Adams said, stepping closer. "There's a dead man here, and you were found at the scene of the crime."

Ted didn't move, kept his stare locked on Adams. "What are you charging me with?"

"Who said I was charging you with anything?"

"That's what I thought." Ted slipped on his jacket. "We done here?"

Adams put the toothpick back in his mouth. "Stay away from Lina." He rested his other hand on his sidearm. "She doesn't need any more confused than she already is."

"She told me you two were separated."

"That's true." He pushed the hat back on his head. "But we're working on patching things up. And she doesn't need you screwing around with her emotions, confusing her."

"Well, we're just friends," Ted said, walking away. "But the way I see it, Lina has a mind of her own. She can do whatever she wants."

"I didn't say you could leave yet."

Ted continued walking. "You know where to find me if you need me."


Ted pulled another rock from the top of the wall and eased it to the ground. Judging from the expanse of missing stones, the opening would be wide enough for his truck to drive through if he needed it to. He couldn't believe how long it had taken him to remove thirteen stones from the top row. It wasn't just that they were heavy, the grout was the most unrelenting substance he'd ever encountered.

Wiping his forehead, he stole another glance at Myrtle before reaching for another stone—his first attempt in the row beneath the top one. He was used to the extreme amount of exertion needed to remove those from the top row and was surprised that the first in the next row was slightly easier to move.

His thoughts drifted to Gary's mutilated body, bringing a bout of acid reflux with it. He'd tried calling Earl a few times since the funeral but got no answer. He wanted to give him his grieving space. After all, he knew what Earl was going through, and he didn't want to make things worse for him.

He stared at the wall, forcing his mind to clear. He knew this was a vulnerable tactic, but he had to move the bad away. He closed his eyes to welcome the quiet, and that was when his thoughts turned to Lina. He couldn't get over how gracefully she had aged since he'd last seen her. Her smile was the same one that prompted him to ask her to the junior prom. Realizing he was grinning, Ted flipped the stone off the wall and onto the ground.

Something shiny caught his attention within the exposed mortise. He brushed debris with his fingers and found a metal object covered in dried mud. He first mistook it for a heavy coin, but quickly realized it was somewhat oblong in shape. He took it to the kitchen faucet to rinse off the caked earth. Once the water flowed over the thing, an image began to emerge. *An angel*? He used the old toothbrush Myrtle kept by the sink for hard-to-reach dishwashing crevices, and recognized developing words amid the mire. SAINT MICHAEL, PATRON SAINT OF PARATROOPERS, PROTECT US. Then he brushed his thumb across the pendant loop at the top.

"Teddy?" Myrtle's voice sounded stronger than it did the night before. "Everything okay?"

"Everything's fine," he said, drying the item with a dish towel. "Just found something interesting."

Myrtle was trying to sit up when Ted entered the room. "What is it?" Her gaunt appearance startled him.

"Some kind of a medallion," he said, handing it to her. Her eyes seemed set further back in her head. "Found it inside the wall. . . between stones and mortar."

She donned her glasses and squinted at the piece. "Upon my honor to God," she said, her gaze never wandering from the piece. "Daddy always was superstitious."

"You think he put it there?"

"I'm sure of it." She smiled at the object. "He was always carrying these around."

"What is it?"

"Protection." She finally turned her attention to Ted. "The archangel Michael was the patron saint of Paratroopers. Daddy said Saint Michael protected them from harm." She smiled at the medallion as though she were gazing into the eyes of her late father. "Daddy was one of the Army's first paratroopers during World War One."

"Why would he put it in the wall?"

"Who knows." She handed it back to him. "He probably thought it would protect those of us in the house."

"Protect?" He studied her face. "From what?"

She shrugged. "Like I said, Daddy was superstitious."

"I guess so."

She turned her gaze out the window. "Looks like you're making some progress."

"The stones were really tough to move at first, but they get a little easier with each one I bring down."

She smiled. "It's seems like you've been working on it forever."

"I've never seen anything like it. The mortar seemingly fuses the stones together. . . as one big stone."

Daddy said he'd learned about interlocking stones and super mortar while stationed in Europe." She raised her eyebrows. "Said you had to treat the stones with some kind of chemical before applying the mortar."

Ted held the medallion out to Myrtle. "Here, take this."

"I'd rather you keep it."

Ted shook his head. "It belonged to your father."

"Daddy had dozens of 'em, Teddy. I want you to have this one." She put a hand on his. "Besides, I'm willin' to bet you're gonna need it worse than me."

\* \* \*

Ted pulled on the steel toed boots and reflector striped clothing before walking into Jerry's office. "I suppose I'll be considered a red hat for a while," he said, tucking the denim shirttail into his work pants.

"Not at all." Jerry opened a desk drawer, retrieving a slightly scuffed black helmet. "You have more experience than most of our underground crew, plus you've had

far more than the required forty hours of safety training."
He tossed the helmet to Ted. "Of course you'll eventually
have to attend more training to get acclimated with the
latest technology." He handed Ted a helmet light. "But, as
of this moment, you are good to go."

"That's great."

"I am going to partner you with a veteran, though."
His gaze was prodding. "Just to make sure the rusty spots
get oiled safely, if you know what I mean."

"I do," Ted said. "And I appreciate the gesture." He
allowed a smile to surface. "Lord knows after twenty
years, I've got more than a few rusty spots."

"I'm going to put you with Leo," Jerry said, writing
something on a blank timecard. "That all right with you?"

"Of course."

Jerry glanced up from the paperwork. "He was the
one who requested it, just so you know."

"Leo has always looked out for me."

Jerry handed the timecard to him. "You gonna be all
right?"

"Yeah, no problem." He rubbed the back of his neck.
"Like riding a bicycle, right?"

Ted tried to keep up as Leo walked through the murky
depths of the mine like it was his own backyard, singing
old Hank Williams songs. His pace was quick and deliber-
ate—a little too brisk for a man his age. . . and far too
brisk for Ted.

"I thought you were going to retire," Ted said. "You
were supposed to move to Florida and fish away the rest

of your life when you turned sixty-five."

Leo shrugged. "The economy messed that up."

"Well, the fish should be thanking their lucky gills."

"You got that right," Leo said, laughing. "For now, at least."

Ted's light flickered a few times, prompting him to check the connections. "These newer shafts are huge."

"Yeah, we're now cutting them twelve feet high and twelve feet wide."

"Wow, that's amazing." Ted scanned the enormous passageway. "We've passed several sections. Where are we going to be working?"

"We're gonna walk from section to section, checking the lifeline and escape boxes," Leo said, pulling his gloves on. "It's a good way for you to get familiarized with each safety station."

"Sounds good."

"Looks like someone's at the next station," Leo said, pointing toward a light in the distance. "Let's check it out."

They found a miner, maybe in his late thirties, sitting near a first aid box with an outstretched splinted leg.

"Randy?" Leo said, kneeling in front of him. "Are you okay?"

Perspiration beaded the man's forehead. "Think I broke my leg." He winced when he tried to move. "Everett put this splint on me before goin' to get help."

Leo shook his head. "What happened?"

"We were movin' roof beams," he said. "Everett and me were trying to set one when it slipped out of my hands and landed on my leg."

Leo looked as though he could feel the pain. "You're lucky it didn't take you out."

"Almost did," Randy said. "I moved fast enough to get out of the way, but this leg was planted."

"Come on." Leo motioned for him to stand. "Let's get you topside. There's no telling how long Everett will be getting help."

Randy grabbed Leo's hand and grunted as he rose to his good foot. "The pain's not as bad as it was earlier. I was afraid I was going to pass out at first."

Leo turned to Ted. "You all right to stay here in case Everett and the crew gets all panicked when they get here and can't find Randy?"

"Sure," Ted said.

Leo put the man's arm around his neck. "We're gonna take our time walking as far as we can."

"I don't think I can do it."

"You'll be surprised at what you can do when you try," Leo said, winking at Ted. "Just let the bad leg hang, slightly bent, and use me as a crutch." He turned back to Ted. "I'll be back as soon as I can. There's water in the packs, stay hydrated."

"I'll be fine."

The noises from the men faded in the distance, along with their lights. Ted's footfalls were muffled when he finally moved toward the ready packs, sounding as though recordings on a tinny speaker.

He found a bottle of water and drank deeply. The light from his helmet flickered, casting long shadows through the cavernous expanse. *Better find a backup before this one goes out.*

He searched through one of the packs, astonished at its disarray. There seemed to be no rhyme or reason as to how items were stored. . . . The whole thing resembled a plundered toy chest. *Has Jerry seen this mess?*

The light flickered again just as a rumbling grew in the distance. Ted paused, listened. The noise echoed through the passages, making it difficult to pinpoint its origin or direction.

His stomach clenched, perspiration penetrating his shirt. It was not a sound he'd ever heard before in the mines. . . and he'd heard the worst. As best he could guess, the ruckus was coming from section eleven. *There's no such thing as a Mothman.*

The flickering worsened until the light eventually went out. By the time it came back on, the distant noise was growing closer. He dug into the pack, frantically searching through lifeline accessories, leather gloves, tools, rebreather masks, and first aid items. The flickering continued until the light went out again, urging him to ransack the items in the box blindly.

The noise morphed to monotonous thumps the nearer it drew—then stopped several feet from the station. Ted stood silent again, trying to detect movement. A shuffling on the floor made him flinch as it sounded as though someone, or some *thing*, was moving toward him. A wave of nausea came over him when the sting of sulfur reached his nostrils.

He started digging into the pack again, still listening

for hints of where. . . whatever it was might be. His fingertips finally found a familiar handle, and he pulled what he was sure to be a flashlight from the mess and turned toward the shuffling. The noises inched closer as he fumbled for a switch. He wasn't sure if the sounds had ceased or if he could no longer hear them over his hammering heart.

Aiming the flashlight forward, he waited a moment, listening. Hearing no sound, he pushed the switch and flinched at the enormous red eyes reflecting in the light's beam just a foot away. The thing screeched, revealing piranha-like teeth, and lunged forward.

Ted swung the flashlight at the creature's face and tripped over the box behind him in an effort to retreat. The impact of his fall jarred the flashlight out of his hand, sending it banging across the shaft floor. The light's beam danced and spiraled before pointing just to the left of the creature.

A cold wave washed over Ted as he lay motionless among the pack items. He struggled to breathe, his mouth dry as gauze, the back of his head radiating with pain. At first he thought the creature was gone but then heard the rapid breathing, subtle snorts, and shuffling. Sulfur burned his nostrils again as something on the floor slid into the light's beam.

He blinked hard, hoping to quail the blurriness and realized he was looking at an enormous foot with three chipped claws. Something in the pit of his stomach warbled, sickening him. But he knew it wasn't his stomach—it was something. . .

*Blood.* He realized that's what the fly-lighting sensation was on the back of his head. Amid heavy shivers, his eyelids grew heavy, threatening to close. *So cold.* He quietly slipped his hands into his pockets for warmth and found the familiar oval shape he'd found in the wall.

The blurring faded with darkness.

## Chapter Thirteen

Ted opened his eyes, instantly remembering what happened. He shivered as echoes moved through the passageway. He tried to sit up and was rewarded with pain radiating in the back of his head. Touching the spot, he found a small gash with drying blood caked in his hair.

The flashlight was still on the ground, its beam in the same direction it was before he passed out. Although there was no clawed foot this time. . . thankfully.

Light beams moved around him as shuffling drew closer. Then he could hear voices echoing with footfalls. The sourness in his stomach eased the closer the men came. A light shone directly into his face made it impossible for him to see who was there. "Are you all right?" Everette's voice sounded surprised as he moved the light out of his face.

"I'll be fine."

One of the other men handed Ted his helmet. "What happened?"

"I'm not sure." Ted tried to stand on wobbly legs. "Something attacked me."

The men gave one another furtive glances before quietly helping Ted out of the mine.

* * *

Ted declined a trip to the ER for stitches after someone

cleaned the blood out of his hair. Instead, he showered, hoping to wash away all evidence of the coal mine.

Those enormous crimson eyes burned into his memory banks like camera flash floaters, forcing him to recall the attack. He climbed in his truck and discovered a different world than the one he knew just 24 hours prior to coming face-to-face with the monster. It didn't look different, but it was a whole new planet all the same. If something as monstrous as the Mothman could actually exist, then what else was hiding in the shadows of reality? What other truths were lies? What lies were truths? He drove through Coal Branch Hollow as though it was his first trip there—as though he wasn't sure if the road would melt into the creek, or if vampires and zombies would attack at the next curve.

Pulling into the driveway, he wiped perspiration from his forehead. *I just hope she's asleep.* The porch light illuminated the front of the house while a few bugs orbited the single bulb dangling by its own cord. He expected to find a moth among the critters, but saw none as he bound the front steps.

Ted winced as the door screeched open. *Great.* He hoped to quell the squeaking by pushing down on the doorknob while closing the door, but his efforts seemingly worsened the noise.

"Teddy? Is that you?"

He closed his eyes, raking his bottom teeth across his top lip. "Yes, ma'am. Just got home." He took his time removing his boots, placing them next to the door. He stood, listening.

"Teddy? Where are you, honey?"

"I'm here," he said, entering her room. "Are you okay?"

"Fair to midlin'," she said, not bothering to sit up. "Come sit next to me."

She no longer looked like Myrtle. Her tangled hair hung past both sides of her face like coarse curtains ready to close. "Can I get you anything?"

She reached for his hand. "Sing to me, Teddy."

He touched the back of his head. "What do you want me to sing?"

"'Going Home.'"

He cleared his throat, gazing at her frail hand in his. He began singing. The words came from somewhere deep inside him. . . not his throat or diaphragm. His lips tingled with each word, his voice soft, raspy. When he finished, he wiped her eyes with a tissue. "You all right?"

Her bloodshot gaze locked onto his. "You lied to me."

"What do you mean?"

She turned away, tears flowing. Ted crossed his arms over his chest, hoping it would overcome the discomfort the widening silence brought.

"You promised you would never go back into the coal mines." She closed her eyes as if in pain. "And you lied to me."

Ted rubbed the back of her hand, the veins squirming under her thin skin like night-crawlers at his touch. "I'm sorry. I had no other choice."

"What do you mean you had no other choice?"

He leaned back with a deep sigh. "I know about the hospital bills."

She pulled her hand from his. "What does that have anything to do with you breaking your promise?"

"I can't just sit by and watch you lose everything."

Her face flushed. "How many times do I have to tell you? I am dying!"

"I know that!" Ted was shocked to hear his voice raised to that level. "But did it ever occur to you that I will be here when you're gone?"

Myrtle stared at him, eyes wide. "Honey, I—"

"All my life I have lost those I love most." He swallowed hard. "And what do I have to show for it?" Tears came in warm streams. "My mother, my father, my best friend, and now you. Gone forever." A sob hitched in his chest. "And all I have is an emptiness growing inside me."

"What I meant—"

"This has been the only place I have felt safe." His voice softened. "My safe house. I have run from it for twenty years, but I can't lose it. Especially when you're gone." The sobs shook him. "It's my only connection. . . to each of you."

"I'm so sorry, Teddy." She wiped her nose with a tissue. "I've been so selfish. I thought I was looking out for you."

"You've been wonderful," he said, trying to smile. "But you have to understand, the biggest reason I went back into the mines had nothing to do with you or hospital bills—I did it for myself." His gaze dropped back to their hands. "I had to face my fears. I had to do it myself. Or else I'd end up carrying this with me until I die."

Myrtle blew her nose and stared at him. "I understand. I don't like it, but I understand."

He took her hand and kissed her knuckles. "So, how did you know I was back in the mines?"

"I've lived with miners my whole life."

"No, really, what gave me away?"

She pointed at his face. "You forgot to wash off your mascara."

"What?"

"Coal mascara." She gestured to a mirror on the wall. "Take a look."

Sure enough, she was right. Coal dust clung to the edges of his eyelids, creating a mascara-like look that is familiar with all coal miners before they have time to fully scrub. "I see what you mean. It's been a while since I've had to deal with this."

"Baby shampoo is the best thing you can use." She used her fingers to mimic scrubbing her eyes. "Does great, and won't irritate."

"Thanks for the tip."

She stared at him a moment. "Teddy?"

"Yes, ma'am?"

"Just be careful."

"That's the goal."

Myrtle had already fallen back asleep when Kim called to see if Ted had any idea of Earl's whereabouts. It was no secret Earl would have a hard time coming to grips with Gary's death, but no one would have thought the big goof would wind up missing.

*The Waterin' Hole.* Ted slipped his boots on and grabbed his keys. The night air was heavy, pluming his breath as he climbed into his truck. *I'd bet money on him being there.* The Waterin' Hole served as Earl's therapist back in the '90s when he and Kim had the second miscarriage. It was pretty much a laid back place with a handful of regulars and nearly zero drama. Myrtle hated the place, always calling it a "beer garden"—of course, she also called it a "hell hole," "den of iniquity," and a few other choice things. Apparently, the bar's reputation was a bit seedier when she was younger, but the biggest reason Myrtle hated the place so much was probably because her husband, Ted's grandfather, drank a lot of take-home pay there when he worked the mines.

Earl's pickup was in the parking lot along with two older trucks and a '78 Oldsmobile. Ted finished his cigarette before walking in. He chuckled at the thought of having to put out a cigarette before entering a bar. Light reflected from glass fragments on the sidewalk—a broken bottle just a couple of feet from the door.

Stepping inside was like stepping back in time. The place looked exactly as it did when Ted checked in from time to time before moving to North Carolina. Even the barflies were the same—a bit older, grayer, but the same people occupying the same stools.

Earl sat three chairs down from the end with a few beer bottles in front of him. His gaze was frozen onto something invisible on the wall behind the bartender.

"Mind if I join you?" Ted said, slipping into the seat

next to him.

Earl didn't even blink. "Be my guest."

The bartender nodded. "What can I get you?"

"I'll have a coffee. Black."

Earl turned his puffy, bloodshot gaze toward Ted. "I guess Kim sent you to bring me home."

The bartender placed a coffee cup in front of Ted and shook his head when Ted offered a few bucks. "No," Ted said. "She did call, asking if I knew where you were hiding."

"You didn't tell her?"

"Of course not."

Earl turned back to the bottle in his hand. "Thanks."

The coffee was surprisingly weak, and a bit lukewarm. "You doing okay?"

"You know why he stuttered, don't you?"

"Gary?" Ted shook his head. "I just assumed he always did."

"Not at all," Earl said. "It all started when he was around six years old." He took a drink. "He just out of the blue stopped talking."

"I didn't know this."

"He wouldn't look anyone in the eyes, either. It was so weird." He shook his head. "Mom had to feed him the first few days. It was really bizarre."

"I don't doubt that a bit."

"After about six months he started talking again like nothing ever happened, except he was left with that terrible stutter."

"Why didn't you ever tell me this?"

"I didn't know about it until several years ago. Mom made mention of it and told me the whole story." He took another drink. "They had him seeing a shrink and everything."

"Did they ever figure out what caused it?"

"He saw something that scared him is all I heard. Thought he saw a monster and flipped out."

Ted sipped his coffee. "Wow, nothing amazes me anymore."

"I'll tell you one thing," Earl said, sneering. "I've been sitting here, thinking about that thing."

"What thing?"

"You know," he said, looking back to Ted. "The Mothman."

"Yeah?"

Earl finished off the bottle. "It's not what we thought."

"What do you mean?"

The bartender opened another Miller Lite and slid it in front of Earl.

"Well, we've always heard that the Mothman was warning us of tragedy." He took a quick drink. "Or it was offering prophecies to help us."

Ted nodded when Earl stopped, waiting for him to continue.

"I think the Mothman is causing all the pain." His upper lip curled just shy of a snarl. "I think the monster is responsible for all the death and destruction it is *supposedly* warning us about."

"If you'd told me this a week ago I'd have thought

you were crazy. But, unfortunately, I think you are right."

"I tell you what I'm gonna do." Earl arched his eyebrows. "I'm gonna hunt that thing down and blow its head off—big red eyes and all!"

"Earl, you know—"

"This ain't the beer talkin', Ted!" Earl's knuckles whitened on the bar. "Don't you see? If we don't do something, who's next?" His gaze searched the bottle again. "We can't just lay down and let the thing take what it wants."

Myrtle's cell phone rang in Ted's pocket. "I'm not saying that." He answered the phone, finding distinct rustling over the static he remembered from the call he took in North Carolina.

"Who is it?"

Ted motioned for Earl to be quiet. "Hello?" A tingling danced across the back of his neck. "Hello?"

The chorus of unrecognizable whispers repeated every few seconds—in the same tone, same pace. Ted couldn't make out what the stilted whispers were saying, but he knew there was a repeated rhythm, cycle. Clarity came with each repetition until he recognized the words. COME HOME, COME HOME, COME HOME. . . the dial tone broke him from the trance-like state. "Oh, my God."

"What?"

"It's Myrtle."

Earl leaned closer. "What about Myrtle?"

Ted rubbed his forehead. "It's there."

"What are you talking about?"

"The Mothman," Ted said, rising to his feet. "It's at Myrtle's house!"

Ted practically burst through the front door, searching as he moved. "Gran?" Splotches of blood spattered the floor. "Myrtle? Can you hear me?" He entered her bedroom where the bloodied sheets, pillows, and blankets were strewn about the room. The curtains were torn and the hospital bed was shoved against the far wall. "Myrtle! I need you to answer me. It's Ted." His heart was drumming in his ears. "I'm here to help."

A draft of sulfur met him in the kitchen where blood smears marred the linoleum floor. *Where is she?* The opened door moved with the wind, curtains reaching outside as if begging a departed force for mercy. He grabbed the flashlight from the drawer and stood quietly for a moment. He couldn't hear anything out of the ordinary. Following the blood trail outside, he found a path of dead grass leading the section of the wall he'd been pulling down. His legs ached as though his arteries were expanding.

"Myrtle?" The dead grass crunched under his feet. "It's me, Ted." Blood splatter was on the same section of wall he'd been working on. Dirt, leaves, and debris swirled with the wind, bringing with it another wave of sulfur. Something was watching. Something followed very close. Wiping perspiration from his forehead, he slowly scanned his surroundings. He couldn't get over how quiet it was. No crickets. No frogs. Nothing.

He closed his eyes and breathed deeply. *Where can she be?* He was ready to walk back to the house when something inside him refused to move. His stomach rumbled, his legs quivered. He found it difficult to swallow as his mouth was dryer than he'd ever experienced. For a moment he feared he would vomit.

Then something came over him. A clarity he'd never experienced before. Somehow he knew. Tears welled in his eyes as he turned back to the wall and peered over the top. Myrtle's bloodied body lay tangled in the rose bushes.

## Chapter Fourteen

Ted leapt into the bushes, breaking thorny stems from Myrtle's body. She was covered in scratches and bruises, her bloodied night gown in shreds. "Myrtle, can you hear me?" He carried her back over the wall, then knelt in the dead grass, pulling her close in his lap. "Gran? It's me, Ted."

He was about to check for a pulse when her eyelids twitched. "Come on, talk to me." A long exhalation turned to a high-pitched moan, like air releasing from the stretched lips of a balloon. Her eyes opened, but it was clear she couldn't see. "Stay with me. Stay with me."

She turned her face toward him, her gaze frantically searching. "Teddy?" She drew a whistling breath. "Is that you?"

"It's me," he said, caressing her head. "I'm here."

With labored breathing, she edged her face closer to his. She moved her lips but only a whistled breath came forth.

"I've got you," Ted said, gently rocking her. "I've got you."

Tears welled in her eyes as she attempted to speak again.

"Shhh, just take it easy for—"

"Listen," she said.

Ted stopped rocking and leaned closer.

Her eyes widened. "Don't go back."

Her body wilted, her wild-eyed gaze frozen.

"Gran?" There was no reason to check for a pulse. He knew she was gone.

Deep sobs shook his body—he'd held back for so long the release was staggering. Forcing his breathing through his mouth, he focused his efforts on calming the sobs. Tears dripped from his cheeks into Myrtle's hair. "I'm so sorry." He pulled her closer, resting his chin on the top of her head. "I should have been here." The grass crumbled beneath him as he shifted his weight—the lawn's scent reminded him of his baseball glove.

Myrtle had just mowed the day before—just two days after his seventh birthday. Ground Digger Wasps hovered an inch or so from the grass, zig-zagging chaotically. Ted had been begging for a baseball glove so he could play for the Reds when he grew up. Myrtle had loved listening to the games on the radio, and always stopped everything when the Big Red Machine showed up on the single television channel.

She smiled as he tore into the gift's wrapping paper. "You didn't think I'd forget, did you?"

"A baseball glove!"

By the look on her face, you would have thought the glove was Myrtle's gift. "I'd ordered it a while back, but it took a little longer than expected getting here."

He quickly hugged her before donning the glove again, ramming his fist into the leather pocket. "Come on, let's play catch."

"You got it!" She lobbed the ball to him, giving it a

small arch. "Keep your glove held back."

The ball came down, nearly bouncing out of the glove when he caught it. Ted hopped around the yard, arms held up in a victory motion. "I caught it! I caught it! Did you see me?"

"Great job, Teddy!" Myrtle hugged him. "You're my little all-star!"

"Let's play some more!"

"All right," she had said. "Just remember, we don't throw the ball into my rose garden." Her smile had faded slightly. "The ball could do a lot of damage to them." She had smiled again while mussing his hair. "Let me show you how to catch a popup."

Another sulfuric breeze slapped a leaf across Ted's face, jarring him back to his grief. Coldness closed in on him, sending shivers in the noiseless night. The sensation of being watched nagged worse. He couldn't describe the feeling except for a subconscious creepiness. Searching the yard and wall, he did not find anything out of the ordinary.

Then peripheral movement drew his attention to the roof of the house. There, squatted near the edge, was the Mothman, its enormous red eyes staring into him. Ted blanched when he recognized the figure among the shadows. A dozen or so strands of white hair jutted from its bald, misshapen head, moving gently in the breeze. The thing just stared without moving, without making a sound.

"You're going to pay for this." Still rocking, Ted nodded. "So help me, if it is the last thing I do, I will make sure you pay for this."

The creature cocked its head to the side.

"Sit there and stare as long as you want. But I want to you to remember this day—because the day I kill you, I'm gonna remind you."

The creature rose from the kneeling position and flew away. The flapping faded in the distance as the frogs and crickets took up their songs again.

## Chapter Fifteen

Ted sat in the waiting area of the funeral home, looking through a casket catalogue when Kim walked in with Myrtle's favorite dress and shoes in hand. He studied her face, hoping she wasn't about to burst into tears. "Thanks for picking that out."

"No problem," she said, settling next to him. "Are you doing all right?"

"I'm actually better than I thought I would be at this point." He stole a glance at the door. "How's Earl?"

Her eyebrows arched as she released a heavy sigh. "He's still taking Gary's death pretty hard. And now with Myrtle, he's talkin' crazy stuff."

"What do you mean?"

"He's blaming the Mothman for one thing." She rolled her eyes. "And the old fool's been cleaning his guns, swearin' to kill the monster."

"You don't think the Mothman is real, do you?"

"Well. . ." She looked into his eyes. "I'm not one that has claimed to see—"

"It's real."

She reached for Ted's hand. "I am not saying there's no such thing, all I am saying is I have never seen it myself."

"Well, I have. And I know what it has done."

"Do you think it killed Gary?"

Ted shrugged. "I don't know for sure." He pulled his hand away. "But I know beyond a shadow of a doubt, whatever the thing is, it killed Myrtle."

They sat in silence, listening to the soothing piano from the overhead speakers. Kim hugged herself and chuckled.

"What?"

"Do you remember when Myrtle would get in that tiny tent with you, me, and Jeff in the backyard?"

He draped his jacket around her shoulders, pulling it together in the front. "Yeah, we said we were camping out."

"It was so funny how she would get up early to cook breakfast in the house, and then bring it to the campfire like she'd cooked it there."

He smiled. "She always said she wanted to make sure we had an authentic camping experience."

"It's hard to believe," she said, staring at the wall. "All those times in that tent, and the whole time she couldn't handle being confined in closed or tight spaces."

"What do you mean?"

"You didn't know, did you?" She smiled. "I wouldn't have either if Mom hadn't told me."

"Told you what?"

She leaned forward. "Myrtle suffered from claustrophobia since she was a little girl."

"But, she always climbed in that tiny tent with us like it was nothing."

Kim shrugged. "I know. I guess facing her fears to make us happy was more important to her."

"I had no idea."

Kim nodded. "She was an extraordinary woman."

He nodded. "That she was."

The funeral director greeted them with cold hands and a fake smile. He showed them a number of plans with color schemes and prices, then walked them through a showroom of caskets and tombs, offering information on anything they showed interest in.

Ten minutes into the tour, Ted pointed at a plain hickory casket. "How much is this one?"

"It fits in the lower package," the director said.

Kim ran her hand across the finish. "I like it. It looks like something Myrtle would have chosen, if that makes sense."

"I was thinking the same thing." Ted turned to the director. "This is the one."

"If you want to look around a bit, I'll go prepare the paperwork."

The upholstery inside the casket resembled a handmade quilt. "It's a little weird," Ted said to Kim. "Someone who was claustrophobic is about to be sealed in this tiny thing, with a metal tomb over it, and buried six feet underground."

"Where she is right now she'll never have to worry about closed in spaces."

Ted stared at the pillow in the casket, where Myrtle's head would rest. "Thanks for coming, Kim." He rubbed his chin with the back of a hand. "I don't think I could have done this without you."

She put her arms around him. "We'll get through it."

"I know."

"Oh my," she said, touching his face. "That is a terrible scratch."

"Yeah, I must have gotten it while freeing Myrtle from the thorny bushes."

Kim offered a pained expression. "You need to put some of Myrtle's purple medicine on that or it's going to get infected."

"I'll be fine." He pulled the collar away from his perspiring neck. "I just need to get out of here."

"Go on home," she said. "I'll take care of things here."

"I wish I could, but I'd better stay and get it all done."

Kim put her hands on her hips. "You don't think I can handle this?"

"I didn't say that and you know it."

She pointed toward the exit. "Then go on home."

"I just don't want to put you out." He took the jacket she was holding out to him. "Are you sure?"

"Absolutely. I'll take care of everything."

"Tell them I'll be back tomorrow afternoon with a check after I settle up with the bank."

"Okay." She wrapped her arms around him again. "Go get some rest."


Ted walked out of the funeral home and into the cloudy day. The past few hours had been rough. In fact, he was sure he'd throw up at one point looking at caskets, but somehow fought off the nausea.

"Got a minute?"

A police cruiser sat close to the building, as far back as possible. Standing next to it was Sheriff Adams.

"How's it going, Mark?"

"You tell me."

"Not too good at the moment, to be honest." Ted took a Marlboro from the pack, lit it. "Not too good at all."

"Yeah, you've been pretty busy."

Ted took a deep draw, allowing the smoke to do its magic.

"I'm not going to beat around the bush," Mark said. "I need for you to tell me about the night Myrtle died."

"What do you want to know?"

Mark removed his glasses and cleaned the lenses with a handkerchief. "Everything."

"I told you everything when you came to the scene."

"Did you, now?" He put his glasses back on and grinned. "Call it intuition or twenty years on the force, but I think you know more than you're telling me."

Ted dropped his gaze to his feet.

"Surely you're not suggesting your grandmother climbed the wall and landed in the rose bushes on her own, are you?"

Warmth crept into Ted's neck and cheeks. "I told you, that's how I found her."

"I know what you told me." His smile melted. "But I think we both know you're not telling me everything."

Ted tried to read his face.

"What happened, Ted?" He cocked his head. "Did you two get in a disagreement or something? Look, I know Myrtle could be tough to get along with at times."

"Why would I kill a dying woman?"

Mark squinted. "What?"

"Myrtle was diagnosed with terminal cancer." He held back a sob. "She had three months to live. What could I possibly gain by her dying sooner than that?"

"You tell me."

Ted shook his head. "I had no reason to kill her. She was the last person I had in my life! I loved her more than anything in this world!"

"Then what are you not telling me?"

Ted stole a glance at his truck. "You wouldn't believe me if I told you."

"Try me."

"You'll think I'm crazy or on some kind of dope."

"What have you got to lose?" He took a step closer. "I don't believe you as it is. You might as well tell me everything."

"I saw the Mothman."

Mark didn't change his poker face. Didn't move.

"I pulled Myrtle from the bushes and brought her into the yard," Ted said with a dry mouth. "The thing stared at me from the roof as I held her."

"Did it attack you?"

Ted blinked. "No, it flew away after a few moments."

"I see."

Ted rubbed his neck. "It did attack me a few days ago in the mines."

"Is that how you got that scratch?" he asked, pointing at Ted's face.

"No, I got that somehow while pulling Myrtle from

the bushes."

Mark took out a bag of chewing tobacco and stuffed a wad into his mouth.

"I told you you wouldn't believe me."

"I didn't say I didn't believe you." Mark spat behind the cruiser. "But it does make for some crazy talk."

"You think I killed Myrtle?"

"If I thought you'd killed her you would be in a cell right now." He raised his eyebrows. "I just can't figure out how you play into all this."

"What do you mean?"

"I mean you are the common denominator for two related deaths. The marks we found on Gary are the same marks we found on your grandmother." You were at the scene of the crime on both occasions. Can you see where I'm coming from?"

"Look, I have told you everything I know."

"Have you?" He smiled. "Because you said the same thing a few minutes ago—right before you told me about the Mothman. Are you sure there's nothing more you want to tell me?"

Ted stared at his boots. "That's all I know."

"Okay," Mark said, opening the cruiser's door. "But I'm going to warn you, if one more death like this happens with you anywhere near it, I will put you *under* the jail! You understand me?"

Ted nodded. "I do."

"Good." He climbed in the car, rolled down the window. "I'm sorry about your loss, Ted, but I can't neglect my duties as sheriff. I hope you understand that. Just keep in mind, I've got my eyes on you."

Ted watched him pull away and onto the road. "I'm sure you do."

Shadows hung from corners and crevices like stringy moss in the living room. The funeral had been small, mostly elderly friends and family reminiscing about the good old days and how much Myrtle meant to the community. He had feared coming unglued every time someone mentioned Myrtle being in a better place. He knew each person meant well, and the sentiment may have been true, but it still grated against him like nothing he'd heard in his life.

He pulled the tie from his neck and searched for the familiar scent of linoleum and homemade quilts, but could find none. More than likely lost forever as the absence of what made this a home now made it nothing more than a cave. The photograph on the end table was a studio shot of him and Myrtle when Ted was around seven. Her smile was huge—one a photographer never needed to prompt.

Ted closed his eyes, hoping the burning would subside. He touched his shirt pocket and headed for the front door, where the cool air on the porch gently swirled. The night was alive with owls hooting, bats swooping down for whatever bugs were around, and dogs howling in the distance.

He took a seat on the front steps, listening to frogs and crickets harmonizing in the darkness. Warmth entered his face and neck and chest. He balled his hands into fists, pressing a knuckle into his lips. *She's actually gone*. The splashing of the creek was like fingernails raking across a chalkboard. *Yet this hollow lives on*. He closed his eyes, breathing deeply.

"I always feared this day, Gran." He wiped his cheeks. "I knew it would come, but I thought I would be ready for it. I thought not being around you would make it easier." He shook his head. "Now I see it just made things worse. And for that, I'm sorry."

He put a Marlboro to his lips and flicked the Zippo a few times without getting a flame. He shook the lighter, trying again with no luck. "Figures," he said, rising from the steps. "This is turning out to be the perfect day."

From the passenger side of his truck, Ted searched for one of the disposables he kept around for emergencies like this. *They are always in the way when you don't need them.* The scent of stale cigarettes clung inside the truck cab, urging his need to get one lit.

The three cigars from Charlie's nearly fell out of the glove box when he opened it. He removed the Bersa .45 so he could see better. Among bank statements and fast food receipts, the small compartment held the owner's manual for the truck, an issue of *Popular Woodworking*, a box cutter, a roll of Tums, and three disposable Bic lighters.

He held one up to the light to see how much fluid remained. The first flick didn't work, but the second one did the trick. He lit the Marlboro, drawing in as much as he could in one drag. Closing his eyes, he held the smoke in his lungs a moment before releasing. *That's it.* It was like sunshine flooding his insides, driving darkness away.

Something slipped from the magazine's pages when

he tried to return it to the glove box. He hadn't even had a chance to use the cigar cutter yet. It was black with a hole on each end and two blades forming a hole in the center to cut the closed end of a cigar. He almost tossed the device back into the glove box, but held it a moment, staring at it.

He quickly dug the cell phone from his pocket and dialed. "Earl? This is Ted. I need you to be ready tomorrow morning at 8:00 am." He smiled. "We're going to Charleston to see an old friend." He shook his head. "You'll find out when we get there."

## Chapter Sixteen

The truck's heater circulated the cigarette smoke as Ted pulled onto 119 North.

Earl put a dip of snuff in his mouth and spit into the Dr. Pepper bottle he'd brought with him. "What in Sam Hill are we doing going to Charleston so early?"

"I told you, we're going to see an old friend."

"Who?"

Ted smiled. "You remember Charlie Morgan, owns the Squire?"

"The Squire?"

"You know, the cigar shop we used to go to all the time."

Earl spit into the bottle again. "Oh, yeah, I remember Charlie. Good guy."

"One of the best."

"Let me get this straight," Earl said. "You mean to tell me you got me up early to go shopping for cigars?"

Ted laughed. "Not exactly. But let's be honest, it's never a bad time to buy cigars."

Earl spit into the bottle again. "Well, that is true."

"To be honest, Charlie knows a little bit about everything."

Earl's eyebrows met over his nose. "Is that right?"

"But he especially knows about West Virginia myths and legends."

"Okay," Earl said. "What's that got to do with anything?"

Ted leaned his head to the right. "It means we're going to find out how to kill the Mothman."

Ted and Earl found Charlie in the walk-in humidor, putting up new stock.

"Well look what the cat drug in," Charlie said with a laugh.

"Do you remember my cousin's husband Earl?"

"I do." The two shook hands. "Good to see you again, Earl."

"Good to see you, too, Charlie."

"Help us find something new," Ted said to Charlie. "Something bold."

"Let's see. How about these? We just got them in from Gurka."

"Gorgeous," Ted said, taking one from Charlie's outstretched hand.

Charlie pointed at the cigar. "Look how perfect the wrappers are on these."

"These really look great," Ted said.

Charlie gestured toward the coffee table. "Cutters and torches are right there."

Ted pulled his cigar from the cellophane. "Do you have a punch?"

"Sure." Charlie picked up one of the torches. "Right here, on the bottom. It just flips out."

"Perfect." Ted punched the end and lit the cigar. "Now *this* is what I'm talking about."

Charlie smiled. "How's your grandmother?"

"She just passed away," Ted said, handing the torch to Earl.

"Oh, I'm so sorry." Charlie put his hand to his head. "I never met the woman, but I must have talked to her a dozen times or more on the phone when she wanted to know where you were." He let out a soft laugh. "She once threatened to come see for herself when I told her you were not here."

Ted blew smoke toward the ceiling. "She was a tough bird."

"So what brings you to Charleston?"

"We came to see you," Ted said. "We've got a few questions we wanted to see if you could help us with."

"Sure," Charlie said, rising to his feet. "You want to go in my office for a little privacy?"

"If you don't mind, that would great."

"I don't mind a bit." He nodded to the group in the lounge. "Do me a favor and keep an eye on the front for me."

Bookcases lined the back wall in Charlie's office—many filled with old and worn tomes. "You'll have to overlook the mess," he said, slipping into the executive chair behind the enormous desk. "I've been busy helping a friend with a play."

"No problem," Ted said, taking a seat. "This sure is a nice office."

Earl nodded. "I feel like I'm at the principal's office."

Charlie laughed. "Well, you've seen my detention area out there." He puffed at the cigar and blew smoke to-

122

ward the ceiling. "So, what can I do for you gentlemen?"

Ted shifted in his seat, stealing a glance at Earl. "I'm afraid what we have to say may sound a little. . . crazy."

"Let me guess," Charlie said, smiling. "You wouldn't be talking about the Mothman sightings in your area, would you? A lot of people are coming forth from that area saying they saw him."

"That's exactly why we're here." Ted leaned forward. "We have reason to believe the creature killed Earl's brother and my grandmother."

"Really?"

Ted nodded. "You're the only person I know who could possibly give us information about something like this."

Charlie rose from his chair and leaned against the corner of the desk. "This is truly a misunderstood creature." He molded the words with his hands as he spoke. "John Keel wrote the book *Mothman Prophesies*, depicting the creature as part of some type of cryptozoology mystery or even an alien creature from another world."

"I saw the movie," Earl said. "Craziest thing I ever saw."

Charlie laughed. "Well, the movie held barely any semblance to the book." He placed his cigar in the big glass ashtray on the desk. "And a lot of people think the Mothman is the result of a curse Chief Cornstalk supposedly placed on the land stolen by the white men who killed his son—invoking the Cherokee entity known as the Thunderbird."

"I heard about that on some TV show," Earl said.

"But I have always said if Chief Cornstalk was able to invoke the creature, he would have done so long before things got so far out of hand."

"Good point," Ted said.

"But that theory is not taken too seriously," Charlie said. "In fact, the most popular belief is that the creature can predict the future, or prophesy of coming disasters to warn mankind. I guess because so many have witnessed the Mothman before and during a number of disasters."

"Like what?" Earl said.

"Well, in 1967, 46 people died when the Silver Bridge collapsed in Point Pleasant. You also have the Marshall University plane crash from 1970 where 75 football players, coaches, fans, and crew members died in Wayne County. And then there's the Buffalo Creek Flood of 1972 where in a matter of minutes, 125 died."

A pang of some sort twisted in Ted's gut. "My parents died in that flood."

"I remember you telling me," Charlie said. "I'm sorry I brought it up."

"Don't be. I'm fine."

"That's just three events." He reached for his cigar. "Wanna know what they have in common?"

"What's that?" Ted said.

"Witnesses say that for a few days prior to each event, even up to minutes before each disaster commenced, a huge man-like thing with enormous wings was seen flying near the sites with large red eyes."

"I knew it!" Earl said, slapping his knee. "So, you think the monster causes the disasters, not predicts them."

Charlie's eyebrows went up. "Quite the contrary."

Ted shrugged. "I don't follow."

"I don't think the creature is *causing* the events. . . I do think the Mothman is predicting the disasters, however I don't think it is doing so to warn or help humans in any way." He shook his head. "It's not warning us about the disasters. . . I think it is feeding from them."

Earl rose from his chair. "Feeding?"

"That's right," Charlie said matter-of-factly. "I think it feeds on the pain, anguish, and suffering of those dying. . . and especially of the survivors and family members."

Ted stared at the desk. "I don't understand."

"It's a fallen angel," Charlie said. "It feeds off the suffering of humans. It knows these horrible events are going to happen—it doesn't interfere or cause them—it merely arrives in advance and feeds from the aftermath."

Earl sat back down. "So, you don't think this creature can kill?"

"I didn't say that." Charlie took a few more puffs of his cigar. "It has killed in the past, probably more noted, pets. Dogs to be exact. Why? Because people love their dogs, and if their beloved pets are found mutilated, it creates a great deal of pain and suffering in the humans attached to those pets." He shifted his gaze to the floor. "And the same with human deaths, too."

"Tell me one thing," Ted said with a shaky voice. "How do I kill it?"

Charlie offered a crooked grin. "How does one kill an angel?"

"I'm not sure I'm followin' too well here," Earl said.

"When you say fallen angel, what exactly are you talking about?"

"We've all heard how the devil was kicked out of heaven and thrown down into earth, along with his followers, his angels." Charlie's eyes glistened as he spoke. "Supposedly, they were attempting to take over heaven."

Earl shook his head. "I guess I should have paid more attention in Sunday school."

"According to some historians, theologians, and scholars, fallen angels are only allowed to kill humans seven days after they taste the blood of their victim."

Ted closed his eyes. "Oh my God."

"What is it?"

"I found Myrtle bleeding from scratches and bruises, lying in the floor just seven days before she died. She described the creature, but I thought it was because of the medication she was taking. And Gary cut his finger on some piece of glass just seven days before he died." Ted ran his fingertips over the scab on the back of his head.

"Ted?" Charlie knelt in front of him. "What is it?"

"I came face-to-face with the creature in the mines," he said. "I stumbled and fell, blacked out."

"So?"

"I woke up with blood matted in my hair from the fall."

Earl slapped Ted on the shoulder. "You didn't tell me about that."

"When was this?" Charlie asked.

"Four days ago."

Earl squirmed in his chair. "That doesn't mean the

thing tasted your blood."

Ted chuckled. "So, how can we kill this thing?"

Charlie walked behind his desk, eased back into his chair. "Well, Egyptians used a particular perfume during mummification to keep fallen angels away from specific corpses. They used it to protect their own lives as well."

Earl looked as though something was caught in his throat. "Perfume? Are you serious?"

"I'm not kidding," Charlie said. "It's called qeres. I studied it in great detail while helping Kathryn Snavely with her thesis on Egyptian mummification processes. I'm not sure if you remember Kathryn. She was the little girl from Hurricane who sold Girl Scout Cookies to us every year. Gosh, I guess she was around five when you saw her. Anyway, the unfortunate thing is only twelve of the thirteen ingredients for the qeres are actually known today."

"You amaze me," Ted said. "You know that?"

Earl nodded. "Only way you'd be more amazin' would be if you knew the thirteenth ingredient."

"Well," Charlie said, grinning. "I think it's love of one's closest friends."

"Love?" Earl leaned forward. "How could you get love into a perfume?"

"Love has always been thought of as a bond that cannot be broken—here or in the afterlife. For one thing, qeres cannot be used as a one-size-fits-all remedy—it is specifically made for each individual."

"How are we supposed to bottle an intangible?" Ted asked.

"First, you would have to collect blood from your

seven closest friends. The idea of blood brothers actually derived from this, the blood represents the life and love of each person willing to fight for the one using the qeres."

"So these seven are safe?" Ted asked.

"As long as the angel doesn't kill the user." Charlie shrugged. "The qeres has no power once the user is dead, which means the angel will taste the blood of all seven of your loves. . . and I'm sure you can guess the rest."

Ted scrunched his eyebrows down, stood. "Wait a minute. If the creature comes a little early, waiting on a particular tragedy then that means—"

Charlie held his hands outward. "A major disaster is about to hit the area."

"I know where," Ted said, remembering Myrtle's weird phone call about the bear. "There's going to be a major disaster at the mines."

Ted was dialing Myrtle's cell before he and Earl got to the truck. "Jerry, this is Ted." He moved the phone from one ear to the other as he climbed in the driver's seat. "You need to get everyone out of the mine as soon as possible."

"Real funny, where are you?" Jerry said.

"This is not a prank. Listen to me, you need to evacuate every person out of the mine, something terrible is about to happen."

"What?"

"A tragedy like you've never seen."

Jerry sighed. "Have you been drinking?"

"No, I'm not drunk! I just need you to listen to me."

"I am listening. What are you talking about?"

Ted pinched the bridge of his nose. "I'm not sure exactly what is going to happen, but there's going to be some type of disaster there."

"Where are you getting your information? How do you know about this?"

Ted closed his eyes. "It's the Mothman. That thing is predicting tragedy at the mine." He realized he was nearly shouting and brought his tone down a bit. "Look, I know it sounds crazy, but you have to believe me."

"Geez, you *are* drunk, aren't you? You know I can't just shut down the mine for no reason. The owners would have my head."

Ted turned his head until his neck popped. "If you don't do it, the blood of those men and women will be on your hands!"

"I told you I can't just shut down the mine for no reason!"

"You're telling me there's no safety regulation you can go to in order to check things out if you think there might be a problem?"

Silence on the line was broken with another sigh. "I can pull everyone above ground for thirty minutes while running a safety check. But, when the check is finished, I'll have no choice but to put everyone back to work."

"That's all I am asking. Make sure the check is a real check, not just going through the motions so you can get the belts running again."

"All right. You owe me one."

"Thank you, Jerry."

Ending the call, Ted placed the cell phone in the console and started the truck.

"Now what are you gonna do?" Earl asked from the passenger seat.

"I've got to convince seven people to give me blood at the risk of dying."

Earl put another chaw of tobacco in his mouth and leaned back. "You can count me in."

"Thanks, man."

## Chapter Seventeen

By the time they got home, they'd made enough phone calls to secure five people who cared for Ted enough to give blood. "We're getting close," he said.

Earl held to the door handle as they turned on Coal Branch Road. "So far, we have Aunt Dorothy, Kim, Charlie, Jerry, and me."

"We need two more."

"I see one waiting for you," Earl said, nodding toward Myrtle's driveway.

Lina offered a dainty wave from the porch steps.

"What's she doing here?" Ted said as they came to a complete stop.

Earl rolled his eyes. "She's probably going door to door selling Avon."

Lina rose from the steps as Ted approached. "I'm so sorry to hear about Myrtle," she said, tears forming. "She was like a second mother to me."

Ted looked away. "I know."

She laid her head to his chest—wrapping her arms around his waist—as tears and sobs overtook her. "I wish I could take your pain," she said, squeezing him tighter.

He pulled her closer, caressing her back and shoulders. "I'm so sorry, Lina."

"For what?"

"For leaving." He brushed a strand of hair from her

eyes. "I was a coward for ever leaving like I did."

"Ted, you don't have to—"

"Yes, I do." He shifted his gaze to the ground before returning it to hers. "You deserve to hear it. You may not understand, but at least you deserve to hear it."

"Y'all want me to wait inside?" Earl said, pointing to the front door.

"That's not necessary, Earl." Ted didn't move his gaze from Lina. "You need to hear this, too." He lowered his voice. "I lost my parents at such an early age, death seemed natural. But when Jeff died, I lost it. I thought I was somehow jinxed—that the people I was closest to or loved most would die earlier than they were supposed to because of me."

Lina touched his cheek with a gentle hand.

"I know it sounds stupid, but that's why I left," he said. "I didn't want anything to happen to you. I didn't want anything to happen to Myrtle, or Aunt Dorothy, Kim, or Earl. So I ran. I ran and hid."

"It's in the past, Ted." Her smile melted him. "I don't blame you for what you did. It took years for me to understand, but I recognized you were in survival mode."

"But the thing I want you to know is I *never* stopped loving you. That's the hardest thing about it. I felt that I had to distance you to ensure your safety, and the sacrifice was worth it in my mind." He shook his head. "But I never stopped loving you. . . just as I never stopped loving Myrtle or the rest of the family."

"I never stopped loving you, either," she said, tears freely flowing now. "Even when I married Mark. I loved him, don't get me wrong, but I always felt like there was something missing in my life. I knew it was you."

"Well, you're just in time to help," Earl said, stepping closer.

Lina offered a smile. "Help with what?"

"No," Ted said. "Not Lina."

"But you don't have that many friends," Earl said. "You need two more people, and you can't be choosy about who they are."

"I've put her through enough. I pushed her away to protect her, remember? I'm not going to drag her into this and maybe get her killed."

"What about me, Kim, and your Aunt Dorothy? What are we, chopped liver?"

Ted shook his head. "That's different, I didn't ask any of you—you all volunteered to take part."

"Stop!" Lina's eyes revealed the feistiness Ted remembered all too well. "You two act like I'm not even standing here. Tell me what you are talking about, and *I* will decide if I want to take part or not."

Earl briefly explained everything as Ted stared into the hillside.

"Mark has warned me that a lot of people have reported seeing the Mothman," Lina said. "And that I should be careful." She breathed deeply. "You saw this thing?"

Ted nodded.

"And you think it killed Myrtle and Gary?"

He nodded again.

"I want to help."

"Lina, you don't—"

"Just stop, Ted. I want to do this." Tears welled again. "I *have* to do this. She leaned forward and kissed him on the lips. "I love you, don't you understand that?"

"I love you, too. And that's why I don't want—"

"Too late. I've already made up my mind."

Earl grinned. "Now all you need is one more."

Ted turned to Earl. "Would you please go inside?"

Lina pulled closer to Ted. "All I ask in return is one thing."

He brushed a strand of hair from her face. "What's that?"

"When this is over and done with, you have to take me to a beach."

Ted laughed. "Deal."

"I'm not joking," she said with a giggle. "I want to dig my toes in the sand and wade in the water."

"You got it."

Kim was sitting on the porch when Ted dropped Earl off at their house. A heaping ashtray smoldered in the swing beside her. "I got him home safe and sound," Ted said from the truck cab.

"I was beginnin' to wonder." Kim glanced at her watch, an obvious attempt to animate her point. "It's been hours since you called."

Earl laughed. "Ted had a visitor waitin' for him when we stopped to get his checkbook." He climbed out of the truck and ambled toward the porch. "I thought I was back in 1989 at one point."

"Shut up, Earl."

"Really?" Kim grinned. "What happened?"

"You shoulda been there—"

"Shut up, Earl."

Kim rose from the swing, squealing. "Are you serious?"

"Let me put it this way," Earl said, "their lips were doing more than just talkin'!"

"Shut up, Earl," Ted said while driving off.

Lina had surprised him with that kiss. He didn't mind, but he'd worked hard at pushing her out of his brain—to learn to survive without her. Things were different now and he didn't know quite how to handle the situation. Yes, he still loved her, but would it be fair to her to try to pick up the pieces and start over? Would he be able to deprogram his original programming?

Lighting a Marlboro, he rested an elbow out the open window as Johnny Cash sang "Ring of Fire" from the radio. He tapped his fingers on the steering column, singing the few words he knew. A siren began mixing with the mariachi horns from the radio, increasing in volume until Ted checked his rear-view mirror, where he found flashing blue and red lights.

"What now?" The speedometer showed 67. "Great. Just what I need."

The cruiser pulled behind him on the side of the road, lights still blazing. The sun was descending beyond the mountain behind the patrol car in the rear-view mirror, the blending of red and yellow skies with the blue and red lights was strangely hypnotic.

Ted watched for the officer to exit the vehicle and approach. When the man stepped out, he donned his Smokey hat and strutted to the side of Ted's truck. "License and registration, please."

He handed them to the officer. *Thank God it's not Mark.*

"Do you know why I pulled you over?" The deputy was too engrossed in examining the documents to look up.

"I think so," Ted said. "After I saw your lights I noticed I was speeding."

"I clocked you doing 66 in a 55 zone." His expression was blank. "Hold tight, I'll be right back."

*Mark is really working me over.* He watched the mirrors, waiting for the officer to return. *He's not going to leave me alone. And now with the way things are going with Lina, it's only going to get worse.*

The officer finally emerged from the cruiser, again strutting to the side of the truck. "Here you go," he said, handing Ted's driver's license and registration back to him. "And I'm gonna need you to sign here," he said, pointing to the bottom of a citation. "You're just confirming I gave you the ticket."

Ted signed the line and handed the small clipboard back to the officer.

"You have thirty days to—"

Something forcibly hit the deputy, causing Ted to quickly duck to the side.

"What the. . . " The officer was gone. . . as was whatever hit him. "Sir? Are you okay?" Ted searched the area from his cab, afraid to move. "Can you—"

Something slammed into the bed of Ted's truck from above, it felt like he'd been rear-ended by a coal truck. Blurring movement was all he could decipher from the rear view mirror. Turning to look out the back glass, he recognized the mauled young officer lying on his back, trying to keep the monster at bay. Blood spattered the creature, its teeth continuing to rip flesh from the young man's chest. The screams were nails piercing his ears.

Ted scrambled for the .45 in the glove box and exited the truck cab. He fired two shots at the highest vantage of the creature so as to not hit the deputy. "Get away from him!" The thing flew straight up, its screeching fading with distance.

Ted climbed into the truck bed. "Can you hear me?" He put his fingers to the side of the man's neck. "Can you hear me?" He wiped the gore from the man's face and found deep lacerations. Not able to find a pulse on the man's neck or wrist, he climbed down from the truck bed and vomited.

The red and blue lights made the scene look worse. He thought he would vomit again but his clenching stomach produced nothing. He dialed 9-1-1 and waited for an answer. "There's a policeman down near Dempsey Branch," he said. "Send an ambulance."

Ted sat on a metal bench, staring at his boots. Florescent lights flickered overhead, giving the grey walls and black bars an eerie look. The jail cell was small and smelled like urine. He shared the space with an old man who snored like a chainsaw on the other bench. The fingerprint ink stains hadn't washed off completely as the officers had promised—faded, splotchy, they looked like birthmarks. The old man rolled over, jabbering something unintelligible, and plummeted to the floor.

"What'd you do that for?" he said, slowly climbing to his feet. With beady eyes and a shaggy beard, the old coot reminded Ted of comedic cowboy actor Gabby Hayes.

Ted bit his bottom lip to keep from laughing. "Excuse me?"

"Why'd you push me off the bench?"

"I didn't touch you," Ted said.

The old man glared at Ted as he settled himself back to the bench. Dirt and grime clung to his clothes and skin, somewhat of a filth sheen. Officers probably had to wash the old man's hands to get the ink to stick for fingerprinting. "I'm watching you," he said in a low tone.

Ted reached for his pack of Marlboros and closed his eyes when he remembered the officers boxed up all his belongings when they signed him in.

"I ain't afraid of you," the old man said in the same low tone. "I ain't afraid of nothin'!"

Ted ground his teeth, breathing deeply.

"And if you think for a second that—"

"Shut up!" Ted was on his feet before he realized it. "I don't want to fight you, but I will!" He realized he was standing over the old man as he cowered against the wall. The man shielded his face with a shoulder and elbow. Ted allowed his fingers to unfist, his voice dropping to a softer tone. "So just leave me alone, okay?"

The old man didn't say anything. He kept his arms in defense mode until Ted sat back down at his bench. The expression on the man's face was a frozen cry. No tears. No sounds.

"I'm sorry," Ted said. "I didn't mean to go off like that."

The old man didn't move. The fear finally melted from his face, turning to a defeated blank.

"I just lost my grandmother." Ted rubbed his brow. "And a lot of strange things are happening. But that's no excuse. . . "

After a few moments of staring, the old man laid down on the bench with his back to Ted. The snores returned almost immediately.

A dull pang swam through Ted's head. What if I'm here after the seventh day? Would the Mothman come for me here? He closed his eyes, rubbing his temples. Would I be safe behind these bars?

A clanging down the hall broke the silence—followed by jangling keys and footfalls as they came closer. Shadows stretched into the cell as Sheriff Adams stepped in front of the bars with a disdainful expression. After what seemed like minutes, he finally unlocked the door and opened it. "Come with me."

Ted followed him through the maze of corridors and into the sheriff's office where the scent of coffee and something else he couldn't quite put his finger on met him at the door. Stacks of paper cluttered the desk, along with folders, mail, and empty Coke bottles.

"Coffee?" Mark asked, already pouring a cup for himself.

"Sure."

He slid the mug to the end of the desk. "Have a seat."

John Wayne movie posters adorned the walls, each rustically framed. A full-sized saddle on the back table. *Leather*. That's the smell he couldn't identify.

"We take it personal when one of our own is killed," Mark said, sliding into the chair behind his desk. "It's like losing a family member."

Ted nodded. "I know that feeling well."

Mark stared a moment before taking another sip. He looked as though he was ready to speak again but took another sip instead. The florescent buzz overhead mingled with the settling hisses of the coffee maker. "Travis was like a son to me." The quaver in his voice was genuine. "He left a wife and two little girls."

Ted shifted in the chair. "I'm sorry to hear that."

Mark squinted his left eye while raising his right eyebrow. He pointed a remote control at the flat panel TV on the stand. Grey noise erupted until he pushed another button, which brought a pixelated video to the screen. Obviously shot from a dash cam of one of the cruisers, the video revealed the rear of Ted's truck. The young officer walks to Ted's open window, hands him a clip board. And even though Ted knew it was coming, he flinched when the creature swooped in, knocking the officer into the side of the truck before carrying him straight up. Within seconds the two slam into the bed of the truck where the thing is mauling the poor deputy.

Emerging from the driver's door, Ted held the .45 out in front of him like he'd seen every cop on TV do, only he was visibly shaking. Two shots fired and the thing was gone.

Ted shifted his gaze to his hands. "Turn it off, please." He wiped sweat from his forehead and pressed a hand against his stomach, as if the gesture could quell the nausea.

Mark turned the TV off and crossed his arms over his chest. "I owe you an apology."

"I don't need an apology."

"Look," Mark said, rising from the chair. "Travis was one of my best men. He was as straight as an arrow and did exactly what he was told." He paused a moment. "Do understand what I am saying?"

"Sounds like he was a great guy."

Mark cleared his throat. "He was, but that's not what I am trying to say." He placed the coffee mug on the desk and stared at the TV's blank screen. "I had Travis following you."

Ted didn't react.

"You could have remained in your pickup and not gotten involved." He rubbed the side of his neck. "But you risked your life to try to save his." He cleared his throat. "And I want to thank you for that."

"I just wish I could have saved him."

"Me too," Mark said. "You know, I have had so many eye witnesses about that monster and I just disregarded it as people making stuff up." He shook his head as if dismayed. "I have had clues that made no sense—things you only see in a movie, you know?" He shook his head again. "But I never dreamed the witnesses were telling the truth about the Mothman until I saw the video from that dash cam."

"I know exactly what you mean."

"I'm even hearing and seeing things—things that freak me out, but then nothing comes of it."

"What do you mean?"

"I was home shaving about a week ago when I heard a racket on the living room roof. It scared me so bad, I cut myself with the razor. But when I went to check, I couldn't see anything. That monster has turned me into a jumpy ball of nerves."

"It's a demon."

"I know."

Ted reached for his Marlboros, then placed his hands on the desk when he remembered he didn't have them. "I have a plan to kill it."

"I know that, too." Mark's poker face offered no clues. He walked back behind his desk and sank into his chair. "You've been busy." He opened the desk drawer and brought out a vial of blood. "I'd like to help," he said, handing the vial to Ted.

The sudden dryness in Ted's mouth made it difficult to swallow. Warmth moved into his face as a chill tingled up his back. "But, how. . ."

Mark smiled. "Lina told me everything." He shrugged. "I called her after I saw the dash cam footage, telling her what I'd just witnessed, and she explained everything." His gaze shifted to the floor. "I'm doing what

I'm doing because of your actions to save Travis. I don't think I could live with myself if I didn't."

"Thank you," Ted said, waving the vial. "I know it wasn't an easy choice."

"It wasn't." Mark smiled mischievously. "But you should know that vial comes with a stipulation."

"I knew it."

"All I ask is for you to leave Lina alone." Mark's eyebrows inched up his forehead. "And if you survive whatever it is you plan to do, you have to leave town and never come back."

"You act like I'm the one that caused you and Lina to split." Ted shook his head. "You are your own obstacle. She didn't leave you because of me, she left you because of *you*."

Mark leaned back in his chair. "That may be true, but she'll never come back to me with you around."

"What about Lina? Doesn't she have a say in the matter?"

"She does," Mark said. "I'm just narrowing down her choices."

The vial burned in Ted's hand. "I can't believe you're actually doing this."

"Let's be honest here, I'm doing you a favor." Mark put a fresh toothpick in the corner of his mouth. "If you really cared about her, you never would have left her the way you did." A confident grin stretched across his face. "You didn't even say goodbye. You didn't even have the common courtesy to tell her you were leaving."

Ted closed his eyes. "You don't understand, I—"

"You're right about that, Teddy boy. I don't understand. I don't understand how someone can say they love another person enough to ask for that person's hand in marriage, yet care so little about that person's well being that they pack up in the middle of the night and disappear without so much as a 'Have a nice life' or anything."

Ted stared at the floor.

"I might not have been the perfect husband, but I was there to help her pick up the pieces. *I* was the one who gave her a shoulder to cry on. *I* was the one who had to convince her that it wasn't her fault. *I* was the one who kept her from hurting herself."

Ted glanced up at him. "What are you talking about?"

"She didn't tell you?" A look of disgust smeared Mark's face. "A few weeks after you'd left, Lina washed down a handful of sleeping pills with enough liquor to knock out a professional wrestler." He shook his head. "I was lucky I found her when I did. . . another hour and she would have been dead."

Ted's stomach roiled. "I didn't know."

"Of course you didn't know, how could you? You were in North Carolina starting a new life!"

Tears welled in Ted's eyes.

"I won't let you hurt her again. Do you hear me? I won't let you break her into a million pieces and just take off again so selfishly."

Ted stared at the desktop.

"Time's wasting, Teddy boy, what's it gonna be?"

Ted rubbed his brow. "I don't have much of a choice,

now do I?"

Mark pushed the box containing Ted's belongings across the desk. "So, what now?"

"Now we send that thing to hell."

## Chapter Eighteen

The sweet aromas adrift in Charlie's office seemed inappropriate for the ingredients Ted witnessed going into the mixture over a hot plate. He puffed on his second cigar in twenty years, leaning against the desk. "You never cease to amaze me, Charlie."

Charlie looked over his glasses. "Why's that?"

"This is why," he said, waving his hands over the process as if Vanna White. "Seriously, you've got to be the smartest person I know."

Charlie chuckled. "You must not know too many smart people."

"How did you learn to do this?"

Charlie stopped mixing for a moment, pushed his glasses back up the bridge of his nose. "A lot of reading, I guess." He sprinkled in another pinch of some powdered substance and continued stirring. "I do deep research on things that interest me, and many times, like now, I find myself helping someone."

Ted gestured toward the ingredients. "Funny how everything is a powder."

"To be honest, much of what you see here on the desk was not in a powder form when I got it." He wiped his hands with a paper towel. "I put in a lot of hours getting everything ground into the present forms you see."

Ted puffed at the cigar, sending smoke to the ceiling.

"You should have been a pharmacist. You missed your calling."

"I missed my calling, but it had nothing to do with being a pharmacist."

"Oh? Then what was it?"

"I should have been a psychiatrist," he said, grinning. Then pointed to the edge of the desk. "Hand me that wooden spoon."

"Now that I think of it, I believe you would have made a good one."

Charlie's eyes smiled. "I probably would have ticked off a lot of clients by telling them to grow up and quit acting like a bunch of babies."

Steam came from the pan, filling the room with flowers and pine. "You were not kidding when you called this a perfume," Ted said. "It smells just like women's perfume."

"Well, it is a perfume. While using it during the mummification process, ancient Egyptians believed it provided the first sweet breath in the afterlife." He picked up the pan, shaking the contents, before placing it back on the hot plate. "It was believed one could dip a blade or spear head into the qeres, and the weapon would become lethal to an angel. In fact, you don't need a weapon with it. . . if the perfume comes in contact with the creature, it is a goner."

"You talk like there are records of this from the past."

"Some things are passed down verbally rather than written," Charlie said. "Much of what we learn about the qeres, and things like it, can only be learned by asking the right people." He turned the hot plate off and stirred one more time before placing the spoon on a towel. "We need to let this cool a bit."

Ted puffed on his cigar, spat a tiny piece of tobacco that clung to his tongue. "There's something about all of this that is nagging at the back of my head."

"Just *one* thing?"

Ted laughed. "Well, a number of things, but one thing especially." He flicked ashes into the ashtray. "I don't understand why this thing is so focused on me. It has used the phones, my family members, people I work with, where I work—why would this demon single me out of everyone else?" He shook his head. "I mean, if this thing is feeding off the pain and suffering of masses left by disaster, why is it getting so personal with me?"

"That's a good question," Charlie said. "It's possible you were supposed to have died before."

"I'm not sure I am following you."

"When your parents died in the Buffalo Creek Flood, were you supposed to be with them?"

Ted's head became stuffy. "Yes, but—"

"Were you supposed to be in the car with them when they died?"

Ted nodded. "Yes, but I got sick just before they left, and had my grandmother keep me until they returned."

Charlie removed his glasses, rubbed his forehead. "Then it appears the demon had calculated you as one of the victims and not one of the survivors. The demon felt cheated when you were not in the vehicle." He put the glasses back on, raised his eyebrows. "And it is making sure it gets you this time."

"Good," Ted said. "I'm glad to hear I'm not the only one holding a grudge."

"I think it's cool enough." Charlie moved the pan around on the hot plate, watching the liquid. "Hand me your bullets."

Ted removed the clip from the Bersa .45 and started backing out the rounds one by one. "Will that stuff clog up the barrel?"

"I don't think so," Charlie said. "It's now in a thin liquid state, and should dry that way." He took one of the ejected rounds and dipped the tip into the liquid. "There's no need to immerse them or cover the casings, as they will not touch the creature. . . and it will eliminate the possibilities of clogging up or jamming."

The mixture held a thin pinkish hue and was practically unseen on the rounds when completely dried, which took roughly a half an hour before he could carefully return the rounds to the magazine and the magazine back into the pistol.

"Thanks, Charlie." He secured the .45 in the holster. "Let's just hope this works." He made a frightened face. "Or you may be reading about me in the *Gazette* very soon."

"Good luck, my friend." Charlie handed him a fat cigar still sealed in its cellophane. "I want you to do me a favor. After you defeat the demon, I want you to celebrate in style."

"Hang on to it for me," Ted said, hugging him. "We'll celebrate together. Thanks again."

During the drive back to Logan, Ted kept the holstered .45 within arm's reach. *Today makes seven days.* His stomach gurgled. He rubbed his eyes, wishing he'd gotten more sleep the past few days. He had just enough time to get to the house, eat something quick, and shower before heading to the mines.

Led Zeppelin's "Black Dog" boomed from the radio speakers, Robert Plant's voice piercing Ted's chest with every note. *Seven days.* The bitter nicotine from the cigarette's filter coated his tongue. His stomach rumbled with an acidic surge in his esophagus, forcing him to roll the window down in fear of being sick.

The smoke cleared almost instantly, the force of the air nearly taking his breath. In the middle of turning a deep curve, his leg began vibrating. . . then he realized it was Myrtle's cell phone vibrating. Getting the phone out of his pocket without touching the accelerator took some time, but he managed before it rang the fourth time. "Hello?"

"Ted?" The voice was very low. "Someone or something is trying to break into the house."

"Lina? I can barely hear you." He switched the cell to the other ear. "What's going on?"

Fear strangled her voice, hope brought the whispers lower. "There was a lot of banging on the sides of the house, and then on the roof." He could tell she was crying. "I don't know what to do."

"What room are you in?"

There was a pause. "I'm in the bedroom."

"Okay, listen to me. I want you to lock the bedroom

door, push the dresser in front of it, then lock yourself in the bathroom. And don't move until I get there. Don't open the door even if you think whatever it is has gone away. Okay?"

"Okay," she said, breathing heavily. "Please stay on the line with me."

"That's no problem. Just put the phone on the dresser and push it in front of the door. Then lock yourself in the bathroom."

"Okay." The thud from her putting the phone down nearly busted his eardrum. He could hear her grunting. "It's not budging," she said from a distance.

"Keep trying, you can do it!"

A very small scooting sound ended with breaking glass. "I'm sorry, I just can't do it, I just broke a lamp." She didn't make a sound for a few seconds. "Oh, no," she said, in whispers. "I hear something coming up the stairs!"

"Forget the dresser and lock yourself in the bathroom."

What sounded like a small explosion was mixed with Lina screaming as loudly as he'd ever heard. "No! No! Please don't hurt me!" Then harsh sobs faded.

Something obviously moved through the broken door pieces, releasing a screeching growl.

"Lina! Lina! Can you hear me?"

The phone moved and immediately he started getting weird noises like the day he got the call while in North Carolina. Breathing? Whispers?

"You hurt her and so help me, I will. . ."

Static mixed with the weird fax noises pushed

through. Then a softer background noise that sounded more like a breeze. Ted could almost hear the thing breathing. He could almost hear its heart beating. *YOU KNOW WHERE TO FIND HER.* The connection died. Tossing the cell phone into the passenger seat, he changed gears, and headed for the mines.

## Chapter Nineteen

Ted parked as far from the mining offices as possible, keeping to the darker edges of the lot. He didn't want to park directly in front of the substation, but he didn't want to have to walk too far, either. Backing the truck into a space with the least lighting, he sat for several minutes searching for movement or anyone else within eyesight. He put a cigarette to his lips but returned it to the pack almost immediately, fearing it would give away his position. *Almost time.*

A gentle breeze carried a plastic grocery bag toward the main road, its movement reminiscent of a ghost from one of the scary movies Lina loved to watch when they were dating. He glanced at his Timex and put his truck keys in his pocket. Satisfied he would not be seen, he slipped on his backpack, quietly closed the truck door, and walked in the shadows, head down, quietly focusing on every step.

Inside the substation, he resisted the urge to turn on the lights, taking out a penlight instead, and made his way to the back of the building. Stale air rushed over him as he opened the metal door of the power room, seemingly escaping confinement. The room smelled like old motor oil and sawdust, which he found a bit weird since there was no sign of either anywhere.

He shut down the transformers—silencing the underlying hum immediately—and traced his way to the main switch and pulled it out. The quiet was pitch black, cold. Placing the battery end of the penlight between his teeth, he rummaged through the backpack until he found the pistol grip of the portable drill. *Gotta hurry*. Perspiration stung his eyes as he quickly drilled two holes into the sides of the switch and replaced it in the box as if nothing was wrong. Stuffing the drill in his backpack, he policed his work and retraced his steps out.

Once back at the pickup, he stowed the backpack behind the seats and moved the truck closer to the office doors. It didn't take long before figures with flashlights emerged from the building, scurrying toward the substation. He attached the holstered .45 onto his belt and pulled his shirttail out of his pants to cover it. Wiping perspiration from his forehead and eyes, he took deep breaths in hopes of getting his adrenalin back down.

After a few moments, he gathered his things and headed inside. The penlight barely offered enough light to help him navigate the building. There were surprisingly few others in the building—their helmet lights nearly blinding Ted when they came close. Squelching radios echoed in the distance with voices trying to find solutions to the problem.

The locker room was empty, which gave Ted a chance to catch his breath. Old Spice overwhelmed his locker, reminding him of his father. Gordon Browning had had the reputation of being the hardest worker, yet his uniforms were always clean, unwrinkled. He never had a hair out of place and he always looked and smelled as though he'd just splashed on Old Spice after a shave.

Changing into his mining clothes, Ted reattached the .45 to his belt and laced up his steel toe boots. The helmet light was fully charged, which meant he'd have more light time than air time. As long as the ventilation system was dead with the power gone, he had a few hours before he had to worry about breathing.

Shuffling footfalls echoed near the doorway.

"Ah, Ted." Jerry's smile was halfhearted at best. "I thought I heard someone in here."

Ted fidgeted with his helmet. "How long has the power been out?"

"Long enough," Jerry said without expression.

"Are you okay?"

Jerry put his cell phone to his ear, his gaze never leaving Ted's face. "Gus, this is Jerry. Evacuate everyone." A pause. "That's right, send everyone home immediately." He put the phone in his pocket. "On the record, federal law says I have to evacuate the entire mine if we can't get the power to the ventilation system back up within fifteen minutes." His gaze still unmoving. "Off the record, I found freshly drilled holes in the main switch at the substation. It'll be hours before someone else discovers it."

Ted's collar seemed a few sizes too small, sweaty. "I see."

"I'm going to my office and hopefully get caught up on weeks of paperwork." His gaze was sharp, accusatory. "I hope no one is foolish enough to go down there using the master key I lost in all the confusion." He cleared his throat. "Officially, the mine is shut down, Ted, and you should go home." He held out a hand for Ted to shake. "We'll see you tomorrow."

Ted took his hand in a firm handshake. "Sure," he managed. "In the meantime, let me know if you need anything." Something cold, hard was between their hands.

Before releasing the handshake, Jerry pressed the object into Ted's hand until he curled his fingers around it. "Stay safe, my friend," he said, walking away.

Ted knew it was the master key before he opened his hand to look at it. His throat tightened with thirst. "Let's do this."

Since the power was out, preventing him from taking the cart down, Ted paced himself as he walked the shaft. His legs grew tired after the first mile, but he kept going, listening, watching. Everyone had already evacuated so the tunnels were quiet. *Today makes seven days*. He took out the medallion, flipping it over between his forefinger and thumb. "What, exactly, was the old man trying to keep out?" The echoes of his voice caused his skin to crawl. Section eleven was still a long way away, but he'd walked further in the past. He didn't want to go back to that.

Coming up on section five, Ted stopped for water. The first aid area appeared as though time had stood still for fifty years—as though no one had been in this section for decades. Resting on the supply case, his legs burned with heaviness. Nothing would have felt better than to have removed the boots and keep the old dogs elevated for a while. But that wouldn't get Lina back. That wouldn't rid the world of the creature lurking about to feed on humanity's pain and suffering. He took the last drink from the bottle and continued his journey.

Scratching noises echoed throughout the shafts occasionally, as did metallic noises, poundings, creaks, and sometimes what Ted thought were faint voices. He could never tell where the noises came from and he always kept moving ahead. However, he occasionally caught the scent of brimstone. It became fuel in his lungs, making him walk faster toward his goal.

An unexpected light in the distance moved slightly. The light was obviously behind a figure moving about near section six. Ted turned out his own light so as to not be seen, and walked as quietly as possible in the dark. He kept a hand to the shaft wall for guidance—the cold surface chilled that hand, penetrating his body like a virus. The light in the distance moved from time to time, never aimed in Ted's direction, which convinced him whoever or whatever was behind it, did not know he was there. The closer he approached, the slower he was forced to advance. A low mumbling echoed in the darkness, somehow ringing with familiarity.

The silhouette of a man against the far wall of the tunnel, the light focused away from them and Ted. Some sounds coming from the figure were unidentifiable. A radio? A conversation? It took just a few more steps and he recognized the song. ". . . Why can't I free your doubtful mind and melt your cold, cold heart?"

"Leo? Leo, is that you?" Ted quickly moved to the figure.

"Ted?" The man's head turned toward him, shining

the light in his face. "Ted, what are you doing down here?"

Ted flipped his light back on so he could examine Leo. "I could ask the same of you," he said, kneeling beside the old man. "What's wrong?"

Leo smiled. "My ankle. It's either broken or sprained really bad."

"Here," Ted said, handing him a bottle of water. "Get hydrated while I get a better look at your foot. Which is it?"

"Left one." Leo drank the water as if he hadn't had anything in days.

Ted untied the boot laces and gently removed the boot and sock. "It's swollen like a son of a gun," Ted said, replacing the sock. "How did you manage this?"

"Running," Leo said, grunting and sweating as Ted put the boot back on. "Anyone ever tell you that you're rougher than a cob?"

"Sorry." Ted looked him over. "Anything else broken or hurt?"

Leo's bushy eyebrows climbed his forehead. "Like I would tell you now! I'd be afraid you would rip an arm off and beat me with it."

Ted tried not to smile. "Stop being a baby." He looked closer into Leo's eyes. "What do you mean you were running?"

"Well, I could tell the power was out, so I—"

"Don't lie to me," Ted said, his voice raised. "Tell me the truth."

Leo finally met his gaze. "There's something down here, Ted." The quaver in his voice said it all. "I didn't believe it until I saw it today."

"When did you see it?"

Leo shook his head. "God as my witness, I thought the men were making stuff up to get out of work." He wiped at his eyes. "I never dreamed they would be telling the truth."

"When did you see it, Leo?"

"About thirty minutes ago." Leo shook as though coldness would shatter him. "It was heading for section eleven." He moved his gaze to his feet. "And it was carrying somebody."

Ted's stomach burned as though he'd eaten rotten eggs for breakfast—the sudden burps even tasted as such. "Could you see who it was?"

"It was a woman," Leo said. "I'm pretty sure it was Lina."

Ted closed his eyes. "What did you see?"

"She was alive." Ted cleared his throat. "She was screaming the whole time." He rubbed the bridge of his nose with a knuckle. "I took off after them, but I couldn't keep up."

The wall's coldness finally reached his bones. "Which way did they go?"

Leo nodded ahead, toward section eleven. "The section had been sealed, but as I mentioned to you before, it has been broken open for some reason."

Ted stared into the distance where section eleven was. "Will you be okay until I get back?"

Leo stared at him. "I'd tell you not to go," he said in a softer tone. "But, I know you wouldn't listen."

Ted shook his head. "I have to get Lina."

"I know, just be careful."

Ted rose to his feet. "Are you sure you will be all right until I get back?"

"I'll be fine. Just be careful."

Concrete chunks littered the main shaft in front of section eleven's broken seal—piles of rubble, shards, and rocks everywhere. Ted stepped through the enormous hole, finding only a few pieces of broken concrete on the other side. *Hard to believe no one recognized this was breached from inside.* Donning a rebreather, he made his way into the depths, watching and listening for anything and everything.

Something was different in this section—he couldn't quite put his finger on it. Something darker, colder, quieter. More than likely it was just the simple fact that no one had been there in ages. He moved the light's beam over something shiny, revealing spiderwebs in corners, nooks, and crannies—even the very ground seemed softer under foot.

A distant rumbling echoed through the passages, reminiscent of the cave-in that took Jeff's life. The surrounding walls had creaked with falling coal chips, producing enough dust for him to slow down. He'd been away from his post only a few minutes when the signs of trouble became known. He'd heard the men running. . . seen the black dust moving in like death.

His throat had burned from yelling for Jeff. His heart had hammered his chest as he'd run back to his section.

"Jeff? Can you hear me?"

The rumbling had become louder as more black dust settled throughout the passages. Just when he'd been ready to turn and look elsewhere, he found a figure sitting on the ground at the other end of the tunnel. Jeff's helmet was in his hands, blood tricking down the sides of his face. His unblinking gaze fixed on Ted's.

Another rumbling quickly turned into a massive cave-in; coal and rock thundered into the shaft as fast and as loud as a train crash—the wall of debris cutting him off from Jeff.

He dug at the debris until his fingers bled. He tried to get Jeff's gaze out of his head before darkness took him.

Another rumble down the shaft brought him back to the task at hand. Lina was down here somewhere, and he had a demon to kill.

The scent of brimstone penetrated the rebreather mask, forcing Ted to squint into the growing dust storm. He picked up the pace, fearing he would be cut off from Lina if he didn't make the extra effort. In doing so, he tripped on something, falling hard on his side. The ground was not as soft as he thought, after all.

Quickly rolling over, he crawled back, directing the light at the lump in the middle of the tunnel. The corpse—possibly a man—had obviously been dead for a while. The chest region was a mangled mess with clothing and dried flesh shredded to the point they were indistinguishable. There was no blood pooling or signs of a struggle in the shaft. *Why kill them elsewhere and bring them here?* He examined the chest closer. *It's not eating. . . . It's just killing for sport.*

Struggling to his feet, he took a final glance at the corpse and continued his journey. What the creature had done to that poor soul was incomprehensible, yet it had done the very same to Gary and Myrtle. It killed them where it found them, and it only carried off the person back there in the shaft after it killed him. Ted's chest burned just under his sternum, his stomach squalling. Perspiration beaded his face, stinging his eyes. *Please don't let anything happen to her.*

The burning in his abdomen graduated to stabs of pain as though a hand was clenching and releasing his intestines. His breathing came in labored gulps. The light he directed in front of him trembled, his hands shaking, his skin crawling. *Pure evil.* Those were the words both Myrtle and Gary used when describing their encounters with this thing. Whatever it was that moved over him was not letting go. Tears welled in his eyes.

Out of the recessed darkness, thundering wings beat the air as the creature emerged into the light, eyes blazing red, baring teeth with an intolerable screech. Ted started to duck away to the side when the thing hit him like a truck. Enormous claws sank into his shoulders, dragging him a few feet before dropping him. A scream nearly deafened Ted before he realized it was his own voice. The searing pain radiated into his chest and back, spiraling down his spine.

Scrambling to his feet, he turned with the light, finding a blur of a teeth and claws upon him. The thing was trying to grab him, but Ted fought to keep the thing from containing him. The claws were like razors slicing into his flesh as though cutting watermelon rinds with butcher knives. The light flashed from side to side, round about, making it difficult to visually keep up.

A warm breath brushed his neck, making him strike with everything in him. The rebreather mask was in pieces, hanging. Brimstone and burning flesh came from the thing's mouth, nearly choking Ted as he pushed at the monster's neck to keep those enormous teeth away.

Adrenaline took over as Ted began punching the creature in the side of its head while holding its neck with the other—a neck far too large for him to choke with one hand. When the thing moved backwards, he began kicking at its legs with the steel toed boots. It screeched with each kick Ted delivered. Finally the demon towered over him like a heavyweight wrestler tossing a featherweight to the mat. Its wings beat the air as it flew off into the murky depths.

Sinking to the ground, he coughed until vomit came in force. Scratches and lacerations covered his chest and abdomen, his arms were scraped and bruised, but he was ready to move ahead to finish the fight. Removing the rebreather tatters hanging from him, he adjusted his belt and discovered the pistol was gone. Searching the entire area, there was no trace of the gun or the holster. He took a deep breath and limped on into the tunnel.

## Chapter Twenty

The shaft widened into an area that was as enormous as Grand Central Station. With a high, domed ceiling and seemingly no support beams or structure, the expanse was an anomaly. Coal structures jutted from the ground like platforms and spires. As he stepped inside the hall like area, his shuffling echoed around the way, amplified. Using the mining light to look at the ceiling or far walls, elongated shadows stretched and expanded in the edges of the beam.

The air was stale here, more than likely carrying only a small percentage of oxygen—possibly carrying a larger percentage of methane. The stillness and quiet was absolute. . . . It was as if he had gone deaf. He eventually moved his foot to ensure his hearing was intact. This quiet was a death quiet—no underlying hums or piercing ultrasonic ringing.

He walked further into the space, scanning for movement or sound. Brimstone tickled his nose, then burned. There was no active coal dust here, either—just a silence that devoured anything and everything.

Something tiny buzzed by his head and ascended into the cathedral ceiling. As he gazed upwards, searching, the same thing happened again, and this time he caught a glimpse of a yellow blur. Then a melodic trilling echoed across the way as a bright yellow canary landed on a spire of coal just fifteen feet from where he stood. The song repeated with floating notes and chirps.

Ted moved closer as the bird sidestepped, its head turned to the side, watching his every move. He closed his eyes, allowing the music to wash over him—a soothing tonic to his wounds. . . internal as well as external. The mellifluous notes slowly morphed into a thicker sound, as though he were being submerged in water. He couldn't resist the internal drawing, pulling at his psyche. The pain was not gone, but rather sated—a mere itch in the process of being scratched. Dizziness accumulated with movement, becoming a circling-of-the-drain perception.

In the faded distance, screams scratched at his consciousness. Trying to focus on the cries only brought pain back to his wounds. The trilling song seemed to be attempts to overwhelm the screams, but ultimately ended up enhancing them. There was a familiarity to the cries—information he had seemingly forgotten, but knew he'd once known.

"Ted!"

He focused on the voice, tuning out everything else one by one, and opened his eyes. Staggering from the grip of whatever had a hold on him, he nearly collapsed. "Lina? Lina, is that you?"

"Ted! Help me!" The voice echoed distantly.

The chamber was barren of life—no movement, no canary, no Lina. . . although the echoes of her last cry for help lingered in the ceiling's dome. Walking among the platforms and spires didn't help the search efforts. Wet with sweat and blood, his shirt clung to his skin, possibly the only thing keeping the shredded denim from falling from his shoulders.

The silence was broken with a muffled buzzing. No bird above his head this time, or anywhere else for that matter. Then something scurried in his pocket, vibrating in sync with the buzzing. He fished out the cell phone—its ringer barely audible—and stared at the screen. *This is not possible.* NO SERVICE appeared where the service bars were normally displayed. A blank area displaced the caller name or phone number.

"Hello?" His voice echoed throughout the chamber.

The familiar noises came through the receiver—fax like tones, hoarse whispers, and heavy breathing. Only this time someone was whimpering and crying in the background. "Lina? Can you hear me?"

A weird laughter dominated the mixture of noises before settling back to the same sounds. At least it sounded like laughter. Then some kind of ruckus spurred a scream in the background. "No, please don't hurt me!"

"Lina!"

The laughter returned for a moment, then a discomforting quiet. YOU STOLE MY FEAST.

The connection died.

"No, no, no! Talk to me." Ted switched the phone from one ear to the other. "Please, don't cut me off. Talk to me." His heart rate accelerated. "You want me, not her. Let her go." He glanced at the phone's face before putting it back to his ear. "Can you hear me? I'm the one you want, not her." Sobs caught in his chest, tears welled in his eyes. "Just. . . let her go."

The silence pierced him. Warmth spread through his chest, neck, and ears. His jaw hurt from gritting his teeth so hard, and his hands shook. He threw the phone against the closest wall. The device shattered into dozens of pieces. "Answer me!"

The disquiet wrapped around him as brimstone wafted past. Pressing a hand over his abdomen, he gagged.

YOU STOLE MY FEAST. The weird whispers did not echo in the cavern. They were in his head.

"That's right," Ted said, searching the vicinity. "I made them evacuate the mines." He scanned the ceiling. "But you came here for *me*. . . so why don't you just let the woman go?"

A cold breeze washed over him, carrying a more concentrated scent of sulfur. His stomach warbled again, pushing bile into his esophagus. He swallowed hard against the gorge and wiped his mouth. A crashing from the far end of the cavern captured his attention as coal dust billowed from a newly formed coal pedestal rising from the floor.

An odd silhouette towered in the center of the rising stand, light reflecting off the enormous red eyes, and the wings pulled around the creature like a cape. The thing didn't move. Stood perfectly still, watching, waiting. Movement at the figure's clawed feet revealed a body lying prostrate, a woman.

"Lina! Can you hear me?"

The woman rose to a sitting position. "Ted?" Blood covered her face, matted her hair. "It wants to kill us, Ted!"

Her resigned expression was harder to overcome than the actual aches and pains Ted experienced.

"Just sit tight." He eased closer. "Are you all right?"

"I'm cut up pretty bad," Lina said, sobs coming again. "I can't stand."

The creature's gaze burned into Ted, its crimson eyes kindled, never blinking—a motion flickered there, nonetheless. It was a fluid movement or something natural, yet nothing could seem more unnatural. *Flames*. It was as if the eyes were windows of some sort with flames flickering behind them.

Rising into the air from the pedestal the creature circled the cavern ceiling, obviously waiting for the perfect moment to attack.

Keeping an eye on the monster and Lina at the same time proved to be a difficult task. The creature swooped a few times but continued circling as Lina fell back to the lying position. "Stay awake, Lina."

The Mothman's circling was like that of a buzzard, waiting for death to overtake its prey. The smooth gliding seemed effortless, conserving energy for the most opportune time. The gaze of the glowing eyes stayed on Ted regardless of where the thing flew—as if directing light through a magnifying glass onto his very soul.

"Lina? Can you hear me?"

Ted ran to the risen stand while the Mothman continued to circle. His heart pounded hard and fast, bringing a brief bout of dizziness. Sweat trickled into his eyes, down his cheeks, and broke out on the back of his neck.

Lina was somehow different—possibly thicker,

shorter? Climbing onto the pedestal, he held his stomach again as a wave of vomit threatened to erupt. It looked as though her feet had been hacked off at the ankles by something sharp but imprecise. Scorches on her pants and legs suggested the stumps had been cauterized, keeping severe blood loss under control that would have otherwise been mortal wounds. The rising and falling of her chest made him exhale a deep breath.

I JUST WANT TO DIG MY TOES IN THE SAND AND WADE IN THE WATER. Lina's voice was like a recording in his head.

"Stop it!" Ted put his hands over his ears. "Just stop it!"

Items on the pedestal around Lina were intriguing—a bag of golf clubs, an open tool box, a steering wheel, a police Smokey Bear hat, and an unearthed section of a rose bush. Acid pushed further into his throat. Then his gaze found his pistol, safely holstered and intact. Turning to catch a glimpse of the creature's whereabouts, he knew it was too late to duck as the thing was on him, slamming him from the pillar.

His back hit the floor, temporarily knocking the wind out of him. The creature was on him within seconds, again ripping at him with its claws. The flames in the eyes were real fires burning with red, orange, and yellow. Sulfuric breaths were hard to escape with the thing growling in his face, its teeth threatening to rip through his neck and face.

The pain in his shoulders returned as the claws sunk into his flesh again, lifting him from the ground. In the air, going around and around with dizziness and motion sickness, Ted tried to grab the creature when it let him go. Landing on a coal spire, he slid down its delicate structure as the whole thing collapsed around him. The pain in his shoulders seemed worse this time.

He struggled to his feet, dodging the swooping creature again and again. Landing a few feet away from him, the monster came closer, towering over Ted by at least two feet. It clawed at him, missing its mark several times as it crept closer.

Ted kicked at the thing's legs, connecting once with a steel-toed boot. He staggered back after the kick, taking a defensive position.

The creature released an ear-piercing screech and shot into the air, circling again. *It can be hurt.* It was not invincible after all. But that did not mean Ted didn't need his gun with qeres-dipped rounds. Stiff from the hard fall, he made his way back closer to Lina's pedestal, watching the Mothman continue to circle. He needed an attack plan to give him enough time to retrieve the handgun.

Cold entered his legs and crept into his chest. The blood loss must have been more significant than he'd originally thought. A shiver seized him momentarily, sending jolts of pain through his torso, shoulders, and arms. Then a warming heat washed over him almost immediately. Whatever was left in his stomach was determined to get out. *I've got to get Lina to a hospital as soon as possible.* He rubbed the back of his neck and waited for the thing to attack again.

Easing to his knees, he kept his gaze upward while silently feeling around the ground for palm sized coal chunks or rocks. With two decent sized pieces in hand, he clambered back to his feet, continuing to watch and wait.

Dust stirred around his legs, rising into a quickly dissipating billow. The Mothman swooped a little closer than normal, circling again. Ted gripped the chunks of coal in his hands, watching. The creature made another swoop, this time closer than the last, right where Ted was waiting for it. He threw one of the coal pieces as hard as he could, catching the monster square in the chest, which dropped the thing from flight in an instant.

The monster was on its feet, lunging for Ted without hesitation. Ted barely had time to throw the second chunk of coal before it was on him. This time his aim was off, missing its head by inches.

The Mothman grabbed Ted's wrists while cocooning both of them with its enormous wings, squeezing them together. Barely able to breathe, Ted struggled to keep from blacking out, his strength draining away from him bit by bit. With the tips of his boots just barely touching the ground, he began kicking the legs of the creature, making sure the steeled toes connected with every strike.

The creature tossed Ted to the ground and quickly stepped back. Frantically gulping at the air, Ted sat up, coughing. Before he could take in the second big breath, the Mothman landed on him, knocking him back to the ground. Ted grabbed the thing's pasty wrists but couldn't keep those enormous claws from clutching his neck.

What could have been thunder rumbled across the cavern as chunks of slate-like coal fell all around them. It wasn't thunder. It was a sound Ted knew all too well. Dust and debris rose and fell, a few coal spires and platforms collapsed in the cavern.

The thing's claws clamped tighter around his neck. *Got to. . .* The pressure in his face was incredible—in fact, he was surprised his bulging eyeballs hadn't already popped out. He tried pulling the claws away, digging to get his fingers under the thing's grip. A distant explosion shook them violently, agitating more dust and debris.

Cold seeped in as the light slowly faded. The creature's grunting and snorting were more from exertion than anything, but they were terrifying nonetheless. Ted's eyelids grew heavy as his stomach wailed. He wanted to kick, or punch, or throw an elbow, but his body was deserting him. He eventually closed his eyes, the guttural noises fading.

The sunshine was too bright even with his eyes closed, yet warmed his face as he lay still. A nearby brook babbled with birds singing and a crisp breeze carrying the scent of honeysuckle and blackberries. Still adjusting his eyes to the light, he rose to his feet, taking in the enormous field he was in.

A woman's laughter erupted just over the hillside, out of view. The deeper resonating voice of a man spoke, but Ted couldn't hear the words. He quietly moved closer, craning his neck to see and not be seen. In what appeared to be a picnic, a man and a woman sat on a checkered blanket on a small flat on the hillside

Something about the couple intrigued him—something familiar. The woman was handing sandwiches to the man as he told some story of an adventure he'd experienced earlier that day. A large basket and a glass pitcher of lemonade with large ice cubes were between them on the blanket. There was a faint echo to their voices. The woman turned to face Ted, but she was looking past him or through him, as if expecting someone. Her face was in every photo album Myrtle owned. *Mom*? The man momentarily glanced in the direction as well. *Dad*? Ted's legs became cold, weak. His heart pounding.

"Where am I supposed to sit?" The voice came from behind, startling him. Tears welled in Ted's eyes as Myrtle walked by with a platter of salmon cakes. It was obvious none of them could see him.

Myrtle handed the platter to his mother and knelt to the blanket while Ted's father poured lemonade for each of them. A gentle breeze caught a corner of the blanket, turning it inward.

"What are you doing, Ted?" The voice was soft, calm, somehow separate from this world.

Tears spilled onto Ted's cheeks, his legs growing weaker. "I wondered where you were," he said, keeping his eyes on his family.

"You know me. I like to keep to myself."

Ted turned and stared a moment before putting his arms around Jeff. "I'm so sorry—"

"Hold on, now" Jeff said. "We don't have much time. And there's a few things I need to tell you." He put a hand on Ted's shoulder. "First of all, there was nothing you could have done to save me, or to have prevented the accident. Nothing."

"I know, but—"

"Just listen to me." A smile crept across his face. "You have to let me go."

"What?"

"You have to let me go. Please."

Ted glanced at his hands, surprised to find them clean of blood, scratches, or cuts. "Why are you able to see me but they aren't?" he said, nodding toward Myrtle and his parents.

"Because you and I are not here."

Ted focused on Jeff's eyes. "What do you mean?"

"There's no time to explain."

The sunlight quickly faded, taking Jeff, Myrtle, and his mom and dad with it. The scent of honeysuckle and blackberries, the salmon cakes and lemonade—all gone within seconds. Darkness returned with the heaviness of pain and suffering. Something shuffled in front of him, disturbing the ground. The air he sucked in burned like alcohol in his windpipes, making him cough a few times before opening his eyes.

He nearly dropped the light when its beam revealed Jeff—his body and features a beehive of transparent white noise—detaining the Mothman from behind. He had obviously pulled the creature off Ted, dragging the thing a few feet away. It bared its steady row of teeth, its eyes flaming red.

Ted sat up, nearly choking on another deep breath. Getting to his feet was a bigger challenge than he'd anticipated as he staggered a few steps before finding solid footing. Jeff was nodding toward Lina and the large pedestal, apprehension masking his expression. He nodded again, harder, signaling for Ted to move.

When he reached the top of the pedestal, Ted checked Lina's pulse and pulled blood-caked hair from her face. The sounds of a struggle grew in the direction of Jeff and the creature. A screech echoed through the chamber as another explosion rumbled through, leaving dust and debris.

Ted removed the .45 from the holster almost at the same moment the Mothman escaped Jeff's hold. The thing took flight again, its wings beating the air. Searching the domed ceiling, Ted held the gun out, ready to fire.

The creature was too far away and too fast to waste even one round on. It made erratic circles in the expanse, speeding up and slowing down. The rumbling became louder as portions of the cavern collapsed on the far end. Dust and coal fragments came down like sand in an hourglass around him as the rumbling moved overhead.

Ted checked on Lina while still keeping an eye on the creature. Another rumbling at the far end turned into a huge crash as portions of the ceiling came down, blocking the tunnel he'd used to get to the cavern. Coal dust rolled in like a wave of black fog, engulfing them. The pedestal shook, rocked.

The creature swooped past, the trail of its wings brushing the side of his face. Coal dust coated his tongue, caked his nostrils as he tried to breath. The thing swooped again, this time close enough to slice into his arm with one of its massive claws. The wound burned as blood soaked into the shredded shirtsleeve. Rumblings, crashes, and wings beating the air were all around, moving, twisting.

Trying to focus on the creature had him moving and searching faster than he thought possible. He stumbled, dizziness overwhelming him, and knelt beside Lina, taking deep breaths.

The rumblings faded after a few moments, structures settled with cracks and pops as rubble trickled to the ground in several locations. The dust began to clear, but there was no sign of the Mothman, or Jeff for that matter. The silence was hypnotic, soothing. Crawling next to Lina, he checked to make sure her breathing was normal, she wasn't bleeding, and that nothing would prevent him from moving her. He pulled her into his arms, keeping the pistol in his right hand ready to fire if needed.

He eased down the pedestal, ensuring the footing for each step he took was solid. He positioned his body and Lina's so if he fell, she would land on him and not the other way around. Chunks of coal and rocks spilled down the side of the structure with them. He scanned everything, keeping vigilant of an attack. *Jeff was here.* By the time he got to the ground level, perspiration had covered his face, neck, and back.

"Put her down!" The words echoed as if across a canyon. Sheriff Adams stood at the entrance where debris had seemingly blocked access.

"Mark, thank God you're—"

"I'm not going to tell you again," Mark said, stepping closer. "Put her down."

Ted eased Lina to the ground, putting the .45 down first, and gently placing her head to the hard surface. "She's in bad shape, we have to get her out of here before that thing comes back."

"Dear God," Mark said kneeling beside Lina's legs. "What have you done to her?"

"It was the Mothman. I barely got her away from it."

Mark glared up at him. "Why did you bring her here?"

"The Mothman brought her here."

"Is she. . ."

"Just get her to a hospital," Ted said. "I'll stay here and finish what I came for."

Mark rose to his feet. "I've got a better idea," he said, pointing a 9MM at Ted. "Why don't I just give you a permanent restraining order right here, right now?"

Ted held his hands up in surrender. "Don't do it, Mark. Let's talk about this."

"Talk about what? Talk about how you've destroyed my life? Look what you've done, Ted, she's. . . she's useless now!"

Ted's left eye twitched. "Useless?"

"She's no longer the woman I married! Look at her!" He waved the gun toward Lina. "What am I supposed to do with her now?"

Ted dropped his hands to his sides. "Have you lost your mind?"

"You did this on purpose, didn't you?" Mark aimed the gun at Ted's chest. "You knew you couldn't have her, so you made sure no one else could."

Ted shook his head. "I can't believe—"

The creature hit Mark from behind, swooping him up and away. His pistol flew past Ted's head, landing somewhere behind him. Trying to follow the screams with his light, Ted caught glimpses of wings and dangling feet. The hairs on the back of his neck rose when the screams turned to gurgling.

The creature dangled Mark high above the broken pedestal, its claws deep into his shoulders. The gurgling stopped, replaced by rips and squishes as the monster used the talons of its feet like a cat scratching with its hind legs, slowly digging at the abdomen. Blood, strings of flesh, and entrails draped from Mark's body, slowly gobbing onto the pedestal in a heap.

An iron stench lingered, reminding Ted of the slaughterhouse Myrtle bought pork shoulder and beef round from every other Friday. Ted always accompanied her to help carry the meats wrapped in brown grocery bags and twine. Myrtle always dabbed a little toothpaste under his nose before entering to keep him from getting sick.

Ted felt his way to his .45 and picked it up. With shaking hands, he took aim, his heart thumping his chest vigorously. The Mothman dropped Mark's body in the same split second Ted pulled the trigger. A dual ringing did very little to mask the echoing bang from the .45. The creature flew off into the darkness as Mark's body came down onto the steaming pile with a splat.

The sudden quiet smothered Ted as he watched and waited. He lifted Lina into his arms and carried her through the maze of coal spires and pedestals. Her ragged breathing seemed to grow weaker by the minute, rattling her chest with gulps and wheezes. Perspiration sheened her cooling skin.

The beating of wings returned, carrying the scent of hellfire and damnation.

Then something moved in the distance toward the collapsed tunnel, giving him reason to place Lina on the ground. The light revealed the reflected red eyes of the Mothman possibly twenty feet away. Ted briefly glanced at Lina, making sure to not step on her, and found the creature now just ten feet away when he returned his gaze. His trembling hand held the gun at his side.

THE WOMAN MAY GO FREE. The hoarse voice was in his head again. The creature's mouth did not open, its expression unchanging. IF YOU SURRENDER.

"That's very generous of you," Ted said, trying to smile. "But she can't exactly walk out of here on her own, now can she?"

The thing stared blankly, unmoving. THE WOMAN MAY GO FREE.

Ted stepped forward. "You have to promise to leave her alone." He pointed at the creature. "And that she is safely delivered to a hospital."

The pause was arduous.

IT WILL BE AS YOU ASK.

"I'm going to make sure of it." Ted aimed the gun at the creature's chest and squeezed the trigger. The bang was still echoing in the cavern when the monster burst into hundreds of moths swarming off into the depths of the shaft. "Now go to hell."

Jeff stood several feet away, his body the consistency of swirling cigar smoke. The soundless form drifted closer, adamantly pointing to an opening on the side of the chamber.

"I wish I had more time," Ted said, digging in his pocket. "But I have to get her to the hospital."

Jeff nodded.

"I do want to thank you, though." Ted held up the script coin before placing it on the pedestal next to him. "For everything."

Jeff smiled, slowly evaporating, wisping away.

Ted Picked up Lina and headed through the opening. The rumbling had by no means stopped, but there were no other explosions or falling chunks of coal and debris. Dust filled the tunnel, causing the light to reflect back into Ted's eyes like high beam headlights on a foggy road.

When the thigh of his right leg became numb, Ted placed Lina on the ground and sat beside her. His lungs burned, his arms ached. He wiggled his foot, moving his leg to get the feeling back. *Got to keep going.* Perspiration stung his wounds, mixing with blood, caked on coal dust, and tatters of his shirt.

Lina groaned, her eyelids fluttering.

Ted stroked her cheek. "Are you okay?"

Her face slowly puckered, tears forming.

"It's all right." He brushed a strand of hair away from her eyes. "Everything is going to be fine."

"Where is the. . . Mothman?" she asked in a raspy voice.

"We don't have to worry about that anymore."

She smiled. "You killed it?"

"Yes."

She winced, her smile switching to a grimace. "I've never experienced anything like it in my life."

"Are you feeling all right?"

"I can't move much," she said, touching her brow. "But my feet hurt more than anything."

*She doesn't know.* Ted willed his gaze from straying to her seared stumps. "You'll be fine once we get you to the hospital."

"Mark is going to be surprised," she said, offering a pain-wracked grin. "He didn't think you would make it back alive."

"We better get moving," he said, preparing to pick her up. "Are you ready?"

"I think so."

She screamed when he picked her up, her face contorted from pain. "I'm sorry," he said. "I'm trying to be as gentle as possible."

Ted's arms began losing strength as he walked, he didn't want to stop, but he didn't want to drop Lina either. He shifted her weight higher, moving his arms in different positions. Perspiration beaded her forehead and her lips were turning a bluish gray when she passed out again.

He stepped up his pace. Let's see if we can find Leo.

\* \* \*

The stitches in Ted's chest and abdomen itched against his tee shirt as he entered Lina's hospital room carrying a newspaper he'd bought in the gift shop. It may have been twenty-four hours since he helped Leo and Lina out of the mine, but Ted still caught himself glancing at the skies from time to time.

He pulled a chair next to Lina's bed and eased into it. She'd lost a lot of blood before and after the surgery, which left her weak and unconscious most of the time. After recutting the stumps, building adequate skin graphs, and closing wounds, the doctors were confident Lina would pull through.

The room was quiet and dim. On the wall next to the door was an antibacterial foam dispenser, which was not surprising as these machines were installed almost six feet apart throughout the entire hospital. Red and pink spots marred the thickly wrapped white gauze on Lina's stumps, obvious *weeping wounds* as Myrtle called them. Lina's breathing was normal and her skin and lips were regaining natural color.

Ted opened the newspaper, revealing a story about the mine disaster. Jerry Price was being heralded as a hero for evacuating when he did, saving the lives of hundreds of men and women. Thankfully there was no mention of Ted, Leo, or Lina, or any of the other victims, buried in the section. However, another headline revealed the Logan County Sheriff's department is reporting Sheriff Mark Adams as missing.

Lina moaned. Her eyelids fluttered, opened.

"How are you feeling?" Ted said, folding the newspaper.

She sighed. "I feel like every part of my body has been torn away and then sewn back together."

"Trust me, I know the feeling."

Tears brimmed her eyes. "At least you still have *all*

your parts."

"I see they already told you the news." He moved from his chair to sit on the edge of the bed. "I want you to know I did everything I could."

"I know," she said, wiping her eyes with the palms of her hands. "It's just a little overwhelming right now."

"Can I get you anything?"

"No, I'm fine."

He took Lina's hand in his. "Mark was there."

"What do you mean *there*?"

"I mean in the mines," he said, glancing at their hands. "In the huge room where we fought the Mothman."

She tried to raise up, grimaced, settled back into the pillow. "What was he doing there?"

"He came to help you."

"But how did he know. . ."

Ted shrugged. "He must have followed me."

"I'm surprised he hasn't already stopped by to check on me."

Ted turned his gaze to the window.

"What's wrong?" She squeezed his hand.

"Mark's dead." He put his other hand on hers. "He died trying to. . . save you."

"Oh my gosh." Her eyes teared up again.

He handed a box of tissues to her. "I'm so sorry."

"He wasn't perfect, but I know he loved me."

Ted dropped his gaze to the floor. "I don't doubt that a bit."

A knock at the door startled them both. "I hope this

is not a bad time," Charlie Morgan said, holding up an arrangement of flowers. "These are for the beautiful one in the room." He raised his eyebrows at Ted. "And, no, I do not mean you."

"Oh, they're beautiful," Lina said, struggling to sit up.

Charlie placed the arrangement on the table next to the bed. "I'm glad you like them." He hugged Lina, shaking his head. "My gosh, you haven't aged a bit, have you?"

Thanks for stopping by, "Ted said, reaching his hand across the bed for a shake.

"Hey, look at this," Charlie said, gesturing at the three of them. "A Rose between two thorns!"

Lina laughed. "You're so sweet, Charlie."

"Thank you, ma'am." He nodded toward Ted. "Would you mind if I borrowed this fella for a minute or two?"

"Not at all," Lina said, smiling. "Just be sure to bring him back."

"Don't worry, I won't let him out of my sight."

An ambulance was backing up to the hospital's front doors when Ted and Charlie walked outside. The warm evening hummed in the background along with a chorus of crickets. A couple of EMTs opened the back doors to the ambulance and pulled an empty gurney out of the bay, wheeled it inside.

Charlie reached inside his jacket, retrieved a cellophaned cigar. "Here you go, my friend."

"Thank you," Ted said. "You didn't have to drive all

this way to deliver a cigar."

"I didn't. I know you're still trying to catch your breath after everything that has happened, and I know you haven't had time to actually sit down and think since Myrtle's passing, but I wanted to see if you would be interested in coming to work at the cigar shop."

"I know what you're doing," Ted said with a smile. "I'm gonna be fine."

"I know that. But I could seriously use the help."

"I appreciate your kindness, but I have a job."

Charlie's face puckered as if he'd caught wind of something foul. "You're not thinking about going back in the mines, are you?"

"I am." He put a hand on Charlie's shoulder. "I'm no longer living in the past. It's a safe mine, good pay, and it keeps me home."

"As long as you are happy, my friend," Charlie said. "That's all that matters to me."

"Thanks, Charlie." Ted hugged him. "It's good to have friends."

## Chapter Twenty-One

Ted stared at the rose garden through the section of wall he'd finally finished tearing down. Spring brought new blossoms, and he'd taken the time to prune and lay mulch for each bush, talking to them as he worked.

"There you are," Lina said, moving next to him in the wheelchair.

"Good morning." He gestured toward the garden. "So, what do you think?"

"I think Myrtle would have loved this."

He nodded. "But she would have taken all the credit."

"True!" she said, laughing.

He picked up a stone chip he'd missed during cleanup. "It's funny how things change," he said, tossing the shard into the mulch bed. "And how so many things can contribute to that change."

She reached for his hand. "I know."

"Are you okay?"

"I'm fine," she said, holding her arm next to his. "Have you noticed how much our scars are like matching tattoos?"

He chuckled. "You're right, they do look an awful lot alike."

"How about you?" She took his hand in hers. "Are you all right?"

"I am." A gentle breeze made the rose bushes sway. "But because of everything that's happened, I've had to do a lot of thinking."

"I know what you mean." She offered a mischievous grin. "And I am definitely going to hold you to the beach promise." She held her legs out, revealing the heavily bandaged stumps. "I don't need toes to play in the sand."

He traced a finger over a scar on the back of her hand. "We spend most of our life bleeding from a blade that cuts from the inside out." He shrugged. "I'm tired of bleeding."

Tears welled in her eyes. "Me too."

"What do you say we go get something to eat?"

"Sounds good," she said. "What do you want to eat?"

"I was thinking Pizza."

She smiled. "Yeah?"

He pushed her wheelchair toward the truck. "I don't know about you, but I kind of like the corner booth at Giovanni's."

# What others are saying about
## *Return of the Mothman*:

"With *RETURN OF THE MOTHMAN*, Michael Knost manages to effortlessly fuse the gritty, day-to-day existence of blue-collar life with the expansive history of myth to create a superb story that is both grounded in harsh reality yet enmeshed in cosmological mystery. A writer and novel after my own heart. Don't you dare miss this!" — **Gary A. Braunbeck**, author of *Mr. Hands, Prodigal Blues, Keepers,* and *In the Midnight Museum.*

"With *RETURN OF THE MOTHMAN*, Michael Knost breathes a fresh vitality and an unsettling aura of frightfulness into the Mothman legend. Knost's crisp narrative and ability to chill to the marrow of the bone makes for a fascinating and dread-inducing read. My favorite novel of the year!" — **Ronald Kelly**, author of *Undertaker's Moon, After the Burn,* and *Restless Shadows.*

"Deftly drawn characters, riveting suspense, and a legendary monster add up to one of the best horror novels I've read in years. Don't miss it!" – **Tim Waggoner**, author of *The Way of All Flesh.*

"Michael Knost does what the best writers of horror fiction do— he makes the terrifyingly impossible possible. He grabs hold of the supernatural and shoves it in our faces, leaving us gasping and screaming. I'd never read about the Mothman before. Now I'll think twice, three times, or more, before venturing into the wilds of West Virginia." — **Elizabeth Massie**, author of *Sineater, Hell Gate,* and *Desper Hollow.*

"From word one in his new novel *RETURN OF THE MOTH-MAN*, Bram Stoker Award-winner Michael Knost spins a riveting take on the Appalachian myth that doesn't let up until the final sentence is spun. He's concocted a heady brew of horror. This is a story to be read in one sitting with the lights on…as the wings of the strange creature flap ever closer…" — **Pam Andrews Hanson**, multi-published author.

"One thing I love is urban legends. Always have. So I really looked forward to reading Michael's new novel *RETURN OF THE MOTHMAN*. And WOW, wow, what a great and creepy read it was! Get ready, my dear friends. When you hear crashing thunder from above, pray it's not the massive wings of the Moth-man ready to descend upon your soul! Michael has crafted a new twist on this legend, and you're about to be taken for a thrill ride until the very end." — **Charles Day**, Bram Stoker Award® - nominated author of *The Legend of the Pumpkin Thief, Hunt for the Ghoulish Bartender,* and *Deep Within*.

"Michael Knost's *RETURN OF THE MOTHMAN* takes exquisitely-drawn, grittily realistic blue collar characters and sends them on a cinematic thrill ride of horror. I loved it. It adds a grand chapter to the lore of the Mothman." — **Steve Rasnic Tem**, author of *Deadfall Hotel* and *Blood Kin*.

"A creepy, thoroughly absorbing tale with memorable characters and a true sense of menace!" —**Jeff Strand**, author of *Dweller*.

---

1 *The Mothers And Fathers Italian Association,* Borderlands Press, 2003.
2 And all for the princely sum of 35 cents . . . Thinking back, it doesn't seem possible.

## ABOUT THE AUTHOR
# Michael Knost

Michael Knost is an award-winning author, editor, and columnist in the Horror, Science Fiction, and Supernatural Thriller genres.

He has edited a number of anthologies, including the *Legends of the Mountain State* series and *Specters in Coal Dust,* and he currently writes a column for *Shroud Magazine.* Over the years, he has also penned dozens of short stories.

Michael won the 2009 Bram Stoker Award, Superior Achievement in Non-fiction, for his book, *Writers*

*Workshop of Horror*, a collection of powerful articles and interviews on the craft of writing. An international award, the Bram Stoker Award is a recognition presented by the Horror Writers Association (HWA) for superior achievement.

*Writers Workshop of Horror* also won the 2009 Black Quill Award, Editor's Choice, Best Dark Genre Book of Non-Fiction.

Michael has also worked in the radio, television, and newspaper industries, and currently lives in Chapmanville, West Virginia, with his beautiful wife and daughter.

For more information, see michaelknost.com, or woodlandpress.com.

---

Author Acknowledgements: Woodland Press, Keith Davis, Cheryl Davis, Geoffrey Cameron Fuller, Tom Monteleone, Michael Broom, F. Paul Wilson, Steve Rasnic Tem, Ronald Kelly, Tim Waggoner, Elizabeth Massie, Pam Andrews Hanson, Charles Day, Jeff Strand, Brian J. Hatcher, Frank Larnerd, Shelby Rhodes, Grace Welch, Nancy Eden Siegel, Charlie Morgan, the Squire Tobacco Unlimited, my parents Earl and Frances Collins, my mother-in-law Betty Adkins, and the two beautiful ladies in my life—my wife Jewell and daughter Bella.

# WRITERS WORKSHOP OF HORROR

## Edited by Michael Knost

The award-winning *Writers Workshop of Horror*, edited by Michael Knost, includes an unparalleled list of teachers, all experts in their fields of endeavor.

Michael Knost and Woodland Press assembled a dream team of writers, editors, and professionals for this special project. The result is nothing short of spectacular—a volume focusing solely on honing the craft of writing. You won't find anything in the pages of this volume on marketing or submission tips. That's another book for another time. What you will find is solid advice from professionals of every publishing level on how to improve your writing. Although this project is centered on writing horror and/or dark fiction, the principles and advice inside this book will transcend all genres and all forms of writing. You will richly benefit from the information, ultimately improving your craft by bringing polished elements of horror, fear, anxiety, or dread to your work when needed.

Contributors include Clive Barker, Joe R. Lansdale, F. Paul Wilson, Ramsey Campbell, Thomas F. Monteleone, Deborah LeBlanc, Gary A. Braunbeck, Brian Keene, Elizabeth Massie, Tom Piccirilli, Jonathan Maberry, Tim Waggoner, Mort Castle, G. Cameron Fuller, Rick Hautala, Scott Nicholson, Michael A. Arnzen, J.F. Gonzalez, Michael Laimo, Lucy A. Snyder, Jeff Strand, Lisa Morton, Jack, Haringa, Gary Frank, Jason Sizemore, Robert N. Lee, Tim Deal, Brian Yount, Brian J. Hatcher, and others.

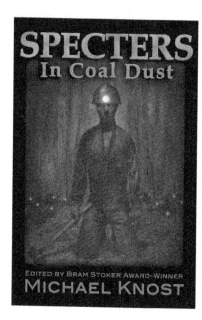

## SPECTERS IN COAL DUST

### Edited by Michael Knost

The depth and darkness of the coalmine has been described as the blackest of black, the loneliest of lonely, and the coldest of c-o-l-d. American miners have tunneled the earth's bowels for the black diamond since the early 1700s, and unexplained tales of ghosts and specters have made their way to the surface with nearly every load of anthracite.

"Then in the trees on the mountain-side of the property, she could hear a breeze picking up, but after only a few seconds she knew it wasn't wind at all, but breathing, difficult breathing, from lungs that never could get enough air. Dark figures appeared in the spaces between scattered trees, carrying lanterns that did nothing to illuminate them." — from Steve Rasnic Tem's "Old Men on Porches."

An eerie collection of coal camp stories from some of the horror genre's finest storytellers, Specters in Coal Dust will leave you cold, lonely, and gasping for air.

Contributors: Gary A. Braunbeck, Christopher Golden, Tom Piccirilli, Steve Rasnic Tem, Elizabeth Massie. Lee Thomas, Ronald Kelly, Bev Vincent, William Meikle, Nate Southard, Joshua Reynolds, Barbara Jo Fleming, Michael Bracken, and Brian J. Hatcher

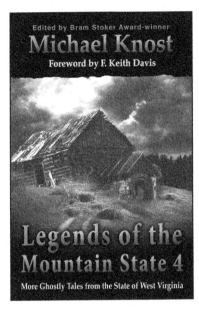

## LEGENDS OF THE MOUNTAIN STATE 4

### Edited by Michael Knost

The fourth installment of the extremely popular *Legends of the Mountain State* series is here. Again, Appalachian myths, ghost tales, and folklore provide an eerie backdrop for powerful, dark, and gritty storytelling.

Concerning the series, *Shroud Magazine* has written that myth, legend, and folklore are among the most powerful forms of storytelling, and *Legends of the Mountain State 4* will not disappoint—not one bit. Michael Knost again takes the reins as chief editor and coordinator. You'll discover thirteen "creeped-out" chapters —bone-chilling tales and legends to delight the reader. Stories are penned by many of the preeminent writers in the horror industry along with exceptional in-state storytellers.

**Contributors include: Gary A. Braunbeck, Steve Rasnic Tem, Alethea Kontis, G. Cameron Fuller, Jason Keene, Elizabeth Massie, JG Faherty, Brian J. Hatcher, S. Clayton Rhodes, Lisa Morton, Mark Justice, Lisa Mannetti, and Michael Arnzen**

## Woodland Press, LLC

For information about special discounts for bulk purchases, contact Woodland Press, LLC Sales at 1-304-752-7152 or email: woodlandpressllc@mac.com.

*Woodland Press can also bring authors and senior editors to your live event, author panel, or convention. For more info, or to book an event, email Woodland Press, LLC at woodlandpressllc@me.com, or visit our website at www.woodlandpress.com.*

\* \* \*

If you are a bookstore or retailer and would like to carry Woodland Press your book titles in your store or online store, contact us about our reseller program. We'd be honored to work with you and your organization.

**Woodland Press, LLC**
118 Woodland Drive
Chapmanville, West Virginia 25508
www.woodlandpress.com
Email: woodlandpressllc@mac.com
304-752-7152

Cover art by Michael Broom.
For more information about the artist, or to see more of his fine work, visit: http://michaelbroom.daportfolio.com.
Michael Broom: Concept designer
michaelbroom.daportfolio.com

CPSIA information can be obtained
at www.ICGtesting.com
Printed in the USA
BVOW04s1309271116
468952BV00001B/14/P